*Praise for* BRATWURST HAVEN

"Often hovering on the cusp of some potential change, the characters in *Bratwurst Haven*'s beautifully written stories share a yearning for more—a better relationship or job or simply a chance to feel content. These all-too-relatable struggles make the stories not only engrossing but also an intriguing and tenderly rendered study of this flawed world we call home."

—Rajia Hassib, author of *A Pure Heart*

"In these twelve linked short stories, Rachel King captures the magic of the American mountain west and the people who call it home. Her characters take work in a sausage factory, pull shifts at a bar to fund their art, struggle with booze and pills, or end up with a haircut after losing at poker. They also care for one another, offering kindnesses both large and small. In *Bratwurst Haven*, King uncovers the complicated ways humans connect, and she gives it to us in prose that is as crystal clear as a bright Colorado day. It is a collection that builds with each story revealing more and more of the friendships and family that bind us all together—and that we cannot escape from, even when we try."

—Wendy J. Fox, author of *What If We Were Somewhere Else* and *If the Ice Had Held*

# BRAT-WURST HAVEN

*Stories*

## RACHEL KING

WEST VIRGINIA UNIVERSITY PRESS • MORGANTOWN

ISBN 978-1-952271-49-6 (paperback) / 978-1-952271-57-1 (ebook)

Library of Congress Cataloging-in-Publication Data
Names: King, Rachel, 1984– author.
Title: Bratwurst haven : stories / Rachel King.
Other titles: Bratwurst haven (Compilation)
Description: First edition. | Morgantown : West Virginia University Press, 2022.
Identifiers: LCCN 2022016269 | ISBN 9781952271496 (paperback) | ISBN
    9781952271571 (ebook)
Subjects: LCGFT: Linked stories.
Classification: LCC PS3611.I58423 B73 2022 | DDC 813/.6—dc23
    /eng/20220413
LC record available at https://lccn.loc.gov/2022016269

The author would like to express her deep gratitude to Jason Frantz, Sarah Munroe, Alex Berge, and Rajia Hassib. She would also like to thank Jensen Beach, Patricia and Philip Brown, Jason Freeman, Sara Georgi, Andrew King, Derek Krissoff, Bryan McKnight, Hailey Piper, Rebecca Rider, Patrick Ryan, Than Saffel, Laura Spence-Ash, Jim Shepard, Rebecca Thomas, Grant Tracey, Joe Truscello, Jeremy Wang-Iverson, Jess Zia, and Olga Zilberbourg.

Stories from this collection were first published in slightly different forms in the following publications: "Railing" in *One Story*, "Visitation Day" in *North American Review*, and "A Deal" in *Green Mountains Review*. The author would like to thank the slush pile readers at these magazines.

The epigraph quotation is from William Kittredge, *Who Owns the West* (Mercury House, 1995), and is reprinted with permission of Jeremy Bigalke, the director at Mercury House.

Cover and book design by Than Saffel / WVU Press

*We are usually bewildered, and mostly capable of transcending ourselves.*

—William Kittredge, *Who Owns the West*

# Contents

———

RAILING / 3

VISITATION DAY / 19

A FRIENDSHIP / 27

A DEAL / 37

POKER NIGHT / 49

CHILDREARING / 59

MURALS / 73

AT THE LAKE / 85

STRANGERS / 97

MIDDLE AGE / 105

PAVEL / 117

BRATWURST HAVEN / 133

# BRATWURST HAVEN

# RAILING

●■●

I got a job at St. Anthony Sausage the fall after I'd been let go from my position as a railway engineer. They'd fired me in May, and I'd spent the summer trying to find a new engineer position in the mornings, drinking at Fred's in the afternoons, and at night watching the presidential primaries and calculating how long it would take for my savings to sift through my fingers. I had child support payments on top of my own expenses, and I liked to treat my favorite bartender, Cynthia, to dinner now and then. Carlos, a regular at Fred's, introduced me to Gus, the owner of St. Anthony, and since the shop was constantly understaffed, Gus hired me on the spot. I earned less than half what I had as an engineer, but it was still a couple dollars over minimum wage. I didn't mind the pay cut because it was temporary: my license wouldn't expire for another three years, and when we elected a president who would push for more gas and oil extraction, railway jobs would once again start to flow.

I liked the physical work at St. Anth. Early mornings, we cut bones out of slabs of meat. Mid-to-late mornings, we poured fifty-pound tubs of meat and spices in a grinder, put the mix through a sealer, and packaged the links. Early afternoons, we packed twenty-pound boxes of links into vans and two guys left for deliveries while the rest of us mixed spices for the next day and cleaned the machinery, tubs, tables, and floors. For the sake of the meat our workroom was cold, and I learned to wear long johns, gloves, and a beanie and was still half-frozen at the end of the workday. But the temperature kept me alert, and the hard work sometimes distracted me from thinking about the man I'd killed.

After the investigation was completed, I didn't discuss it with anybody. I had been officially acquitted, but I kept feeling like there was something I could have done. My train was heading east toward Kansas City. The fog was low and dense. Around 4:30 a.m., I saw something curled up on the rails about three hundred feet away. I put on the emergency brake but knew it was too late. No, I thought. No. Right before, the guy's head rose. I can't remember if I saw his eyes. I later learned he was twenty, and most likely drunk or on something—not that that changed anything. The bang sounded like we'd hit the side of a house. I told the dispatcher to send emergency responders, then got out and ran back to see if I could help a crushed body, because that's what I needed to do.

All ten employees on the factory floor were supposed to do everything, which worked as well as you might expect, especially with no manager and Gus always upstairs in the office doing paperwork with his daughter. This old guy, Joey, had worked there almost forty years and seemed the most likely person to manage, but he usually kept his head down, only speaking to tell a story about old-school St. Anthony—or to tell Gus off. Joey had no teeth and flabby white arms and took a smoke break every thirty minutes. Because Gus's father had promised Joey a salary comparable to what unionized factory workers earned back in the day, he was making fifteen or twenty more per hour than the next-highest-paid employee. If Gus threatened to lower his pay because of his smoke breaks, Joey would threaten to rat on Gus for his violations: he didn't pay us overtime, he only gave us one twenty-minute break in an eight- or nine-hour day, and he dealt with some of his clients under the table. Gus probably figured the more Joey smoked, the sooner he'd die. Rumor was he had cancer.

I was glad Aaron from Appalachia sometimes told us what to do. If we were milling around, he'd say, "Let's move on to the grinder" or "Who wants to help me wash tubs?" If Carlos or my high school classmate Matt were running their mouths instead of cutting, Aaron would glare. Sometimes they'd glare back, but I think we were all grateful someone kept us on task so we could eventually get out of there.

There was Elena, Kathleen, and Honey, the three women, Pete, a Native guy, a couple other Hispanic guys, and another white or two, depending on the week. Enrique, a Mayan Mexican, was the second-hardest worker on the crew. He moved quickly and precisely, listening without comment while we joked and complained, probably because he didn't understand much of what we said. Gus could appear at any time, so we saved most of our bitching about him for the bar. Sometimes we worked without speaking at all, the scrape of our knives or the churn of machinery the only noise.

After I'd been on the job three months, Gus started sending me on deliveries. Thursdays Joey and I delivered to towns north until

Fort Collins; Fridays Carlos and I took the route south toward Denver. It was winter by then, and the delivery van had a bad heater, but I liked to be on the road, the land nothing but flat to the north, east, and south, and to the west until it met the foothills of the Rockies. Trump had won the primaries, and I thought he'd probably win the election. In a year or so I'd be gone, and until then I'd enjoy the drive.

On the last Thursday in March the delivery van kept sliding on 287 between Loveland and Fort Collins. A foot of snow had fallen the night before. I'd had trouble slogging through it to work and had arrived right before Gus let us in at 5:40. If you were late more than once he'd fire you, and I planned to use my free pass for something better than weather. I'd had to dig us out of a drift behind a pizza place in Berthoud, but now we only had three more stops. And I had something to look forward to: Thursdays was my weekday evening with my daughter, Laura. We'd meet at Fred's after school, then we'd walk over to my apartment and make dinner together and hang out until her mother picked her up. Laura and I had a deal: I'd give her hot cocoa with dinner as long as she didn't tell her mom she'd been at Fred's.

We stopped at Larry's, a run-down truck stop, to drop off what we called *rasty*, our grossest product, made from joints, veins, and fat. The dolly wouldn't roll through the snow, so we had to carry in all twenty twenty-pound boxes. After we stacked them in the deep-freeze, Joey looked at the wares while I took a leak. When I came out, I saw him admiring a long-sleeve, gray T-shirt with a wolf on it. "This is sharp," he told me, and bought it, and put it on over his long johns, leaving his coat unzipped to display it.

Traffic was sparse in Fort Collins. No one outside the brick storefronts. Students hurried across the university's snow-covered lawn. We usually unloaded for Oliverio's in an alley between two buildings, but I didn't want to risk getting stuck again, so we pulled up out front. We wheeled the boxes through the main eating area where a manager was doing paperwork at one of the tables. He nodded to us. After five loads we were done. I rested in the van while Joey dropped off the invoice and picked up payment. I was supposed to be shadowing him for that part, but maneuvering through deep snow had worn me out.

The manager came out waving his arms. I followed him back in. Joey lay on the floor, yellow and white foamy vomit splattered next to him across the red carpet. Seconds after I made sure he was breathing, he sat up, wiped his arm across the vomit on his mustache, and collapsed again. The manager asked if he should call someone, and I told him I'd deal with it. I picked Joey up and carried him out to the van. His height made him awkward to carry, and heavy, despite his thinness. The vomit ran from his wolf shirt onto his jeans. His head was slumped over one shoulder.

I remembered the last time I'd thrown up—right after I saw the guy I'd run over. I shined my flashlight along the rails as I ran back. I stopped at what was left of him. Most of his body had been flattened. I turned away, toward the low, black fields. Then I doubled over and heaved three times.

We'd passed a hospital on our way in. "I'm taking you to the ER," I told Joey. I didn't know if he could hear me or not.

As I shifted into gear, the manager ran out again. He had a check in one hand. I rolled down the window and took it. "Gracias," I said.

At a stoplight I opened my water bottle and tossed some water onto Joey's face. He blinked, and I let out my breath. "We're going to the hospital," I said.

He touched the wetness on his face. He looked at his soiled wolf shirt and shook his head. He raised his arms to take it off but then gave up.

I pulled into the emergency turnaround and idled. "Can you walk?" I asked.

"I'm not going in there," he said. He leaned forward and puked on the floor.

"Something's wrong with you."

"I know that." He lifted his arms again and this time managed to wrangle off the shirt. It was inside-out now, and the vomit showed through. He laid the shirt across his lap. "I hope that cleans up."

If it was cancer and he didn't want to talk about it, that was his business. But he needed help. "You should go in."

"Don't have health insurance," he said. He rubbed his hands on his jeans and looked out the windshield.

The inside of the car stank. I rolled the window down a couple of inches. "I'll take you home," I said.

"We'll finish deliveries," he said.

An ambulance pulled up behind me, its lights flashing. I pulled away and back onto the highway. Joey closed his eyes.

By the time I'd finished the Gilda delivery, he was sitting up and smoking with his window open. Snowflakes blew into the cab. I booked it down I-25 and dropped him at his ranch house in Laforge. He stepped out and offered to clean up the mess he'd made, but I told him I'd take care of it.

"Don't mention this to Gus," he said.

It was almost four when I got back to the shop. I stacked the empty crates, cleaned the van, and clocked out. It was cold in the shop, cold outside, and cold in the van, where I'd left the door open so I could smell more than barf and bleach. My legs and lower back and wrists hurt. I'd pulled a shoulder muscle carrying him. I'd worked over ten hours that day and would clock over forty-five that week. Matt had talked about emailing the labor board, and I wished he wasn't all talk and would do it. We all deserved overtime.

They'd been drinking for two hours when I arrived at Fred's. Along the front bar sat a couple of solo regulars who glanced over as I walked in. Cynthia smiled, and I raised my hand. In the back corner, Enrique was playing darts with Laura. Carlos, Matt, and Aaron shared a pitcher at a round table. When Laura spotted me, she ran over, gave me a hug, and said that she was beating Enrique.

"It's about time," I said.

She pulled away. "You smell."

"Worse than usual?"

She lifted her nose. "Maybe. You want to play foosball?"

"Just a minute."

I went to the bar, to Cynthia, who never minded my smell in or out of bed. She had a double Jack neat ready for me. "You look like you need it," she said.

I shrugged. "Bad weather."

"Snowing out there?"

"Something like that."

Cynthia reached across and touched the indent in my chin, then went to the other end of the bar to serve somebody who'd just walked in. I watched the back of her smooth, cream-colored neck. She was only twenty-five. I wondered how much longer I could attract someone that age. I sipped my Jack and walked over to the group. They were talking the usual shit: complaining about how the shop was run and wondering whether Gus was bipolar because he alternated between abuse and praise.

"I thought he was gonna fire Matt just for saying we were ready to go home," Aaron said.

Carlos waved a hand, imitating Gus. "'You'll go when I say you can go,'" he growled.

"Doesn't matter cause I'm about to quit," Matt said. He glowered and gulped his beer. He'd threatened this before.

"If you do, can you call the labor board?" I said. "I'm sick of not being paid overtime."

Matt looked at me, then shook his head. "I need the job, man. Where else would I work?"

"Mountain Sausage is looking for a guy," Carlos said.

"Fuck Boulder," Matt said.

"I heard that, too," Aaron said. "They have benefits. Might look into it."

"Jesus," I said. "If *you* leave, nothing will get done around there."

"Thanks a lot," Carlos said. He stood and headed to the counter.

Carlos was just pissed that Mountain Sausage wouldn't hire him because of his felony. He'd told us how they'd turned him down last summer.

I finished my Jack and poured a beer. "I'll get the next pitcher."

"Smoke break first?" Matt said. I shook my head. I was trying for the third time to quit. I thought about Joey, and wondered whether he'd been chain smoking since I dropped him off. Should I check on him? I looked at my phone to see if I even had his number. Jill, my ex, had texted.

I have to pick up Laura before dinner. Brooke and I need to work at the office this evening and I want to bring Laura with us. We'll get takeout.

I ran a hand through my hair. Jesus. I thought the surprises were over for the day.

Pick her up after the meeting? I asked.

It'll be too late. Do you want her to be tired tomorrow?

My chest tightened. If I wasn't between cars at the moment, Jill wouldn't be able to boss me around like this. I texted that we'd meet her in twenty minutes outside the pinball café.

At the counter, Carlos was tossing back shots with another regular. "Pitcher of Bud," I told Cynthia. As she filled it I asked what she was doing later.

"Here till seven," she said. She grinned as she set down the pitcher.

I figured she might come home with me. It wouldn't be the first time. And if she didn't want to or couldn't, she'd tell me straight out. Carlos brought yet another shot to his lips. I took the pitcher to the table, topped off my glass, and sipped while I stood over the foosball and watched Laura and Enrique spin levers. She smiled as Enrique's goalie scored for her.

"Damn," he said.

"Game point," she said.

They played for another five minutes before Enrique scored. "Good game," he said. They high-fived. At ten, she had an inch on him.

"Your turn," she said to me.

"Not today. Your mom's picking you up soon."

Her eyes widened. "I'm eating dinner with you."

"Your mom has a meeting."

"She can pick me up after."

"It'll be past your bedtime."

"Who cares."

I didn't. I could have told Jill that. "We'll hang out Saturday."

"You said we were going to make sausages and French toast."

"We'll make them Saturday."

She crossed her arms. "I want them tonight."

"You don't always get what you want." I turned away. At the table I drained my glass, set it down, and picked up her backpack. Behind me, she repeatedly spun a lever on the foosball table.

The others had been watching.

"I got a few links with me," Aaron said. "You want them?"

I nodded. "Thanks." Aaron got a package of shrink-wrapped links from his bag and handed them to me. I placed them in Laura's backpack and stepped over to the foosball. "Aaron gave you some links," I said. "If we don't go now you don't get them."

She gave the lever one final, hard spin. I held up the backpack, she slipped the straps over her puffy purple coat sleeves, and we walked outside and down a couple blocks to the front of the pinball café so her mother wouldn't know she'd been in the bar.

Across the street, a couple of girls were making a snowman. Laura watched them. "We can make one Saturday," I said.

"I wanted to make one today."

"Maybe at your mom's."

"With you. Mom doesn't play."

I put a hand on her shoulder. She shrugged me off. Then she looked up, her face alert. "If you don't let me come for dinner, I'll tell Mom I've been going to Fred's."

I felt my whole, sore body tense. If her mother found that out, I'd get to spend even less time with Laura. "Your mom's meeting might go late," I said. "She won't want you waiting for her at my place, missing sleep."

"I can stay overnight."

Maybe she could sleep on a pallet on my floor. Maybe I could be late for work this once so I could help her get ready for school. But I didn't feel like arguing about it with my ex, and I knew fucking Cynthia would make me feel better.

"I have to be at work before you wake up."

"I can get ready alone."

I squeezed her arm. "You probably can. But not tomorrow. I'd have to clear it with your mom when it's not last-minute."

She sighed.

Jill's Saturn pulled up to the curb.

"See you in two days," I said. Laura scrunched her face and said "bye" and got in the car. I waved to her as they drove away.

By the time I got back inside, they'd distributed my pitcher among themselves. "Someone else's turn," I said and looked at Matt.

"Fuck it, man," he said and got up.

"Why'd Cynthia fall for *Lance*?" he asked when he returned with the pitcher.

"I'm not a dick," I said and refilled my glass. Next year, I thought, when I was making more money, I'd get another car so I could drive Laura around.

Across the table Carlos was drunkenly bragging that he had dirt on Dalton Reid, one of the new hires, and the other guys were trying to guess what it was.

"Arson," Enrique said.

"Not paying child support," Matt said.

"Domestic abuse," Aaron said.

Carlos sat up straight, arms crossed, and shook his head after each guess.

"Robbery," Enrique said.

"Bounced checks," Matt said.

"That was you, idiot," Carlos said.

"Knife fight," I said.

"That's Carlos," Matt said.

Carlos flipped us both off.

"Shoplifting," Aaron said.

"Murder," Matt said.

"Nope. It's the worst crime there is," Carlos said.

"Child molester?" Aaron said.

Carlos nodded smugly.

"You're lying," Matt said.

"It's public info. Look it up."

I pulled out my phone and searched for the Colorado sex-offender registry. The new guy was on the list as a class-four felony. "He could have slept with a thirteen-year-old when he was seventeen," I said.

"I doubt it," Carlos said.

"He has kids, man," Matt said.

"You just want someone there with a worse record than you," I said. I don't know why I said it. Maybe because I was worn out and my mind was elsewhere.

"Fuck you," Carlos said. When I looked up from my phone he was standing over me. "You smell like puke."

"We all smell like shit," I said.

"We smell like sausage. You smell like puke."

He was grinning like the asshole that he was. He grabbed my

shoulders and pulled me to my feet. My hurt shoulder throbbed. Blood rushed to my head. I was about to slug him.

Cynthia came out from behind the counter. "No fighting," she said.

"Your boyfriend started it," Carlos said.

"I think you should leave," she said to him. He leered at me. She stepped closer and caught his eye. "Get out or I call the police."

Because of his parole, Carlos wasn't even supposed to be in a bar. He shrugged and stumbled to the front door and out. Enrique went after him with both their coats.

Aaron, Matt, and I sat in silence and finished the pitcher. I stood to get another.

"Last one and then we head out?" I asked Cynthia.

She began to fill it.

"Kid's gone," I said.

"You do kind of smell today," she said.

"We smell every day."

"No. It's something else."

I wanted to tell her about Joey. I imagined him, clothes still on, passed out on a couch in his living room.

She set the pitcher in front of me. "I want to go home and be alone tonight," she said.

I stared at her.

"There'll be other nights."

I didn't think there'd be another night I'd need her as much as this one. "OK," I said. "OK."

Back at the table Matt was talking about Trump. He always talked politics when he was drunk. Aaron dazedly followed his rant.

"He just doesn't want other countries to take advantage of America," Matt said. "The new people here don't understand that because they're the ones taking advantage of *us*. St. Anth was a better town before the yuppies from Boulder moved in and took over all the stores and restaurants. In two years I bet Fred's will be another fucking brewery, or a bakery, or a shop selling candles and Christmas shit. If Trump—"

"Trump isn't Jesus Christ," I said.

Matt blinked slowly. "He might get you your job back."

"Oh, fuck that job."

I didn't mean it. I just didn't want to think about the guy I'd killed, but the mention of that job had me thinking about him hard. I sat down and poured a glass. Both Matt and Aaron were staring at me.

"What?" I said. "What?"

"What's wrong with you?" Matt asked.

It was a valid question. "Just a shitty day."

"What happened?"

Maybe Aaron could call Joey; he probably had his number. "I ran over a guy when I was a train engineer."

"What the fuck?" Matt said.

I told it all. The boy's bones had been pulverized. He looked nothing like a human being. The medics came. Then the police. It had been springtime when it happened, a year ago, and later that morning, as I waited for a replacement engineer, I saw daffodils in bloom.

They watched me closely, struck almost sober. When I was done, no one spoke. After a minute, we took the pitchers and glasses to the counter, raised our hands to one another, and went our separate ways. As I stumbled over the railway tracks and toward my apartment, I wondered whether I should text Aaron to see if he had Joey's number. The sky was blue-black and star-speckled. The snow drifts were deep. I'd see him tomorrow, I decided. Joey never missed work.

I pulled myself up to the second floor by using the stair railing. On the kitchen counter were chicken-sausage links I'd left out to thaw for Laura and me. I warmed up a skillet and dropped them in. Cinnamon and meat scents rose. Under the sizzling, I heard the low moan of a train. I'd also hear one at midnight, and at 5 a.m. I looked forward to the morning, and my routine. I would go through the cold outside to the cold inside. I would unload boxes of meat from the walk-in. For hours, I would cut bones out of flesh.

# VISITATION DAY

On Saturday morning, Elena drank coffee in the kitchen, looking out at the untrampled snow, and thought of her daughter, Nori, who at one o'clock she'd see in person for the first time since her birth, the first time in a month. She'd watched Nori sleeping through the cellphone camera of her ex, who had custody, but that paled in comparison to touching and smelling her. As she rinsed out her mug, the two little boys who lived next door came out dressed in red snowsuits, black stocking caps, and rainbow-colored mittens. She turned up the music on her phone and cracked a window so they'd look up at her, and when they did, she waved at them. They waved back, but grimly, as though they had more important things, such as snowman-making, on their minds.

Elena played Mysonne while she showered. Her counselor had told her to stay away from angrier rappers like DMX. Elena saw her point, but also felt something cathartic in hearing someone articulate feelings she'd had but never had the vocabulary or talent to say like that. She dressed in a maroon turtleneck—she always wore long sleeves now—and skinny jeans. She checked on the boys who'd finished a snowman and were trying to push in a carrot nose that kept falling off. Finally, the younger one, Arjun, grabbed the carrot from the older, Mahir, and stuck it on top of the snowman's head. The creature looked like an alien with a conduit. She thought she could offer them snowman eyes—maybe buttons?—but she didn't have any. As she searched, she decided she'd make cookies and invite the boys up. She'd taken a liking to them the day she'd moved into the unit above their parents' detached garage, when they'd been playing Calvinball from *Calvin and Hobbes*, a comic she'd loved as child. She could also take cookies to her ex's sister, she thought, who'd be bringing Nori to the visitation at St. Anthony Public Library.

The first dozen cookies were burnt, but the second batch was light brown, the chocolate bars she'd used instead of chips melted in strange but beautiful whorls. She made two more batches, then went to find the boys. They were on the snow-covered sidewalk, Mahir pulling Arjun on a wooden sled. They'd taken off their mittens; their hands were red. Elena waved to them, and they waved back.

"Do you want some cookies?" she asked. "I just made some upstairs."

The boys stopped their sled. Arjun hopped off and stepped toward her. Mahir placed a hand on his younger brother's shoulder, pulling him back. "No thank you," he said.

Elena buried her eagerness. "Aren't you hungry?" she asked.

Arjun looked like he was salivating, but Mahir shook his head.

"I'm going to the store," Elena said. "You can go up and get some while I'm gone, if you want."

Elena went back upstairs for her purse, then headed to her Accord. The boys were on the front patch of snow, trying to pull the feet out from under each other. She waved at them faintly as she pulled away.

Elena drove the plowed roads on autopilot. Walmart had always been a comforting place for her. She'd crushed on a girl, a coworker, for the first time while working at a Walmart at sixteen. She didn't tell her mom she was queer, not because she didn't think she'd accept her, but because she worried that they'd stop receiving rent assistance from their church if their church found out. The coworker and Elena used to drive toward the mountains, pull off onto tree-shaded gravel roads, and make out, but Elena didn't have her first official girlfriend until she'd graduated early from high school and moved west to Steamboat Springs. There, she also went on occasional drinking binges. These nights released something in her that nothing else would, something to do with having to lead a double life, to appear straight to her mom and church community. Eventually, she stopped visiting her hometown except at Christmas.

She was attracted to guys, too, though Nori's father, Liam, was the first she'd had a serious relationship with. They'd moved in together after two months, and after six had wanted a kid, which she now found strange, but at the time she'd liked Liam's steady aura and had gone with it. The problem had come while pregnant, when she couldn't go on binges. Throughout the pregnancy a rage grew in her, which she'd let out two months before Nori's due date when she'd cut her wrists.

Today, she walked around the infants' section at Walmart, wondering what her mom would have bought her daughter. Soft things, she thought. Her mom liked soft things. She would have bought Nori the soft blankets, the soft onesies, the soft stuffed animals. Elena touched these objects as she walked by them. Her counselor said it might help her to tell her mom about Nori, but Elena didn't know whether she wanted to admit to her mom why she wasn't taking care of her daughter.

Elena stopped at the infant stocking caps. It was the beginning of winter; Nori might need them. She chose a packet of pink and blue caps with little yellow duckies on them, and in the next aisle found a plastic ducky to match. It would be a few months before Nori could play in a tub, but when that time came, Elena wanted it to be a fun experience.

At home, Elena took the stairs two at a time. In the apartment, only the burned batch of cookies remained on the counter. The boys had taken the others, she thought. She'd said they could come up for cookies, but she didn't think they'd take most of them. Now she didn't have any to give Liam's sister. Anger rushed from her gut to her head. She hurried downstairs. In the back-yard, the boys had pushed cookies into the snowman's face and zigzagged crumbs around the lawn. The streaks of chocolate in the snowman's eyes and its huge cookie mouth that curved above the eyes made the creature look manic. Elena rushed around the house and knocked on the front door.

Arjun opened it. He was eating a cookie. Without thinking, Elena swiped it out of his hand. It fell to the checkered area rug beneath him. Without crying out, as Mahir might have, he leaned over, grabbed the cookie, and gazed at her while munching on it again. By then, his mom Preeti had come up behind him.

"Hi Elena," she said.

She was wearing a neon-green apron. The scent of curry rose

from her. Sometimes, on weekends, she'd make large batches for the entire workweek ahead.

"My cookies," Elena said. "They took my cookies." She imagined the boys jumping up the stairs, Arjun leading. He was probably the one who wasted them, crumbling them across the lawn, while Mahir made the smiley face and eyes on the snowman. She felt her hands fisting and tried to relax them.

Preeti's brow crinkled. "They said you said they could take some." She looked down at Arjun. "Did you not say that?"

"I invited them inside," Elena said. "I invited them in and they wouldn't come."

"Arjun, go up to your room," Preeti said. "Elena, please come in."

The boy stared at Elena's red face before he turned. Elena stepped inside and followed Preeti down the hallway to the kitchen.

A huge pot sat on the stove. On the counter sat a wine glass full of red wine. Preeti turned down the stove, then turned back to Elena, holding the glass.

"I'm so sorry if they took more than they should have."

The scent of onions was making Elena's eyes water.

"They're strong aren't they?" Preeti said. "Would you like to come over later for dinner? We have plenty."

"I don't know," Elena said. "Maybe."

Preeti nodded. "The fact is, I told the boys not to go up to your apartment with you."

"They're welcome to. I don't mind."

Preeti shook her head. "I know you're working through some things. I think it would be best if they didn't."

Anger welled up again. Elena couldn't believe this woman feared she'd harm them.

"You're welcome to hang out with them in the yard." Preeti swished the wine.

What did this lady know about her? Elena thought. Only what she'd discovered through a background check—that Elena was sick enough to have her newborn taken from her.

"Got it." Elena turned and walked out of the room and down the hall.

Preeti followed. "We eat around seven," she said. "We'd love for you to come."

Elena thought of spilling a bowl of hot curry down Preeti's dress, pretending it was an accident. She was as unstable as Preeti thought she was, wasn't she? "Not today," she said.

Back in her kitchen, Elena eyed a bottle of red wine that had been left by the last tenant. She thought of drinking it before she left, how it would help her face Liam's sister, give her a drunk kind of distance. But she didn't want her first visit with her daughter to be like that. If she ever told Nori this story when she was older, she wanted to tell it with emotion and clarity; she wanted to remember she'd been sober. She imagined herself and an elementary-age Nori living in their own house, of them renting out a unit over their garage to help pay the mortgage. If they had a tenant with problems like herself, Elena wouldn't want Nori alone with that person either.

Elena uncorked the wine bottle and headed to the backyard. The red liquid sloshed onto her hand as she galloped down the stairs. She remembered when Liam had found her cutting herself in their tub. She'd left the bathroom door unlocked, probably intentionally, and although she didn't cry out until her third cut, when she did, immediately he was there. The look in his eyes, not of surprise or concern, but of fear, made her dislike him. She disliked him for being scared of this aspect in her.

Outside, she examined the snowman, its strange carrot top and creepy face and no arms, the cookie-fragments of artwork behind him. She wondered whether the boys had modeled it after the grotesque snowmen in *Calvin and Hobbes*. As a child, she'd replicated them: the decapitated heads, the aliens. Her mom laughed at these attempts at horror and sometimes even helped create them. Now, Elena decided to assist the boys in their snow-art. She poured wine on top of the snowman's head, so it looked as though something had stabbed the carrot into it, then dribbled the liquid out of its cookie mouth, as though it were spitting out blood. She followed the patterns of cookies on the ground with wine, until the bottle was empty.

As Elena dropped the bottle into the recycling bin, she heard a tapping on glass. She stepped back and looked up. Arjun and Mahir stood at their bedroom window. She smiled and opened an arm to her additions. Mahir nodded and smiled shyly and waved, and Arjun jumped up and down, delighted, flailing both hands.

When Elena reached the long steps of the St. Anthony Library, ten minutes remained before one. She turned toward the outdoor skating rink across the street, and watched kids and parents skate while listening to Kendrick Lamar through her earbuds. The really young kids pushed a rolling, mini-walker-type contraption that helped them stabilize on the ice. Elena thought this device practical and creative; she'd never seen anything like it. St. Anthony is a perfect little town, Liam, who'd grown up there, had said when they'd met. Like that town in *Hot Fuzz*? she'd asked. Perfect on the surface with bodies underneath? And he said no, not like that. They probably locked up the crazies instead of killing them, Elena thought now. She'd learned that in Colorado you could get a court order to force a next of kin diagnosed as a threat to themselves or to others into long-term, clinical treatment. Elena doubted her mom would do that to her, but she'd feel as though her mom were afraid of her if she even suggested it. She knew that was why she hesitated to tell her mom her situation: she didn't want another person close to her to fear her.

Elena turned toward the glass wall of the library, then walked closer to it. Liam's sister sat on a bench on the far wall, a detachable car seat on the ground facing toward her, away from Elena. Elena imagined Nori dressed in a warm flannel onesie with a hood, and the rubber duckie and stocking caps, compared to a thick onesie and everything else Liam's family had probably given her daughter, seemed rather sad. Elena remembered in the hospital bed holding Nori, her newborn skin against her own newly cut wrists. Her whole body yearned to hold her again, but she didn't want to face Liam's sister. Elena was more likely to encounter pity than scorn from her, but she didn't want to deal with any of it. Elena's breath had fogged up a small spot on the glass. When Liam's sister glanced toward her, she would go in, Elena thought. She would go in, she told herself again. She would go inside in a couple of minutes.

# A FRIENDSHIP

● ● ●

Joey sits with the Ricci boys on a curb. Above them, their parents smoke, the scent settling in the boys' hair. A glint of sun bounces off a trumpet. A clown comes by tossing candy. Joey and the Ricci boys snatch Tootsie Rolls and fake cigars, eat some, and tuck others in their pockets. They pretend to smoke, foreshadowing their futures.

It's the 1950 Main Street Fourth of July parade. Joey is four. The Ricci boys are five and seven. They will take Joey on hikes, teach him how to fish, tease him with garter snakes and gentle punches in their backyards while their parents are making supper. Behind them is an Italian restaurant where Joey's family eats monthly, and on either side of it are storefronts as old as Joey's and the Ricci boys' grandpas, who moved to town to work in a coal mine. But it is the bright sun Joey remembers that day. The sun and the candy. He is not allowed to eat after supper, but that night, before bed, he opens his drawer and sticks his hand in the pocket of his pants, pulls out a candy cigar, unwraps it, and eats it. He stuffs the wrapper deep in the drawer.

When Joey is six, the Ricci boys teach him how to ride a bike. By following them, Joey learns the grids of Old Town St. Anthony, which houses are where and who lives in them. He likes to have this knowledge, he likes how fast he can go from place to place and the *whoosh* in his ears. They all ride downtown to the candy store, stop their bikes, and ogle through the window. The next year, when Joey is earning money delivering newspapers, he parks his bike and uses his earnings to buy sweets. He works as a delivery boy for four years, while his preferences, like the Ricci boys', shift from candy to cigarettes. They smoke together while strolling through the grids of houses, flicking ash on lawns.

When he's eleven, the last coal mine shuts down. Mr. Ricci and his father lose their jobs. The next year is one of quiet panic, when his father paces, when his mother and Mrs. Ricci drive together to Denver for jobs. In the evenings, Mr. Ricci and his dad hang out at the kitchen table writing numbers on lined sheets of paper. They're going to open an Italian American bakery, his mom tells Joey. His dad and Mr. Ricci will bake and she and Mrs. Ricci will run the counter. They'll have a delivery option if he or the Ricci boys want to deliver.

Before the store, Main Street was a five-minute bike ride, a close destination. Now, it's a second home. Before, he knew the candy store, the Italian restaurant. Now, he and the Ricci boys sit on the porch of their families' shop and comment on everything: signs on businesses, styles of shoes, models of cars. Joey loves the soft light of morning and evening, the harsh light of afternoon. He's going up to doors now when he delivers, not only tossing papers from a bike. He encounters women without pantyhose, men without shirts, raucous children, children who seem nervous even in their own homes. His clothes smell like bread and pastries. Even after washing them, the scents remain. At school, a kid makes fun of it, and he and the younger Ricci boy beat him up. Joey keeps the delivery tips under his mattress, saving, though he isn't sure for what.

Joey and the Ricci boys go the shop route in high school. Joey loves spending afternoons in physical movement, not at a desk. He loves learning car mechanics. He decides to save up for a car. He delivers as much as he can. Business is good. At sixteen, he buys a Buick. He drives into the mountains with both Ricci boys, then when the older one joins the Army, with the younger Ricci boy, then when the younger one is drafted, with a girlfriend. He enjoys driving fast, how the air smells clearer up in the mountains. He loves to smoke while he drives along. He makes out with his girlfriend in that car, then breaks up with her the year he graduates from high school, the year the older Ricci boy dies overseas, the year he himself goes to Vietnam.

When the younger Ricci boy comes home with the news of his brother, he and Joey drink and drive together. They speed through Boulder, honking and flipping off hippies. They find waterfalls in the foothills and dare each other to jump into their icy pools. They don't discuss the older boy, but somehow, Joey hopes this helps. When Joey's drafted, he sells his car to someone who wasn't. He puts the money in the bank, telling himself he will come back to it.

After two tours, he returns. The younger Ricci boy is also back. They hang out again, at Fred's, a new pub off Main Street. They play pool and drink some, Joey less than Ricci. Ricci tells war stories. Joey avoids talking about it. If you want to forget something, he thinks, you need to not discuss it. Joey has more of a temper since he returned, and although he regrets this, he simply catalogues it as something that has changed about him, something he has to deal with. He and the younger Ricci discuss their parents' shop, and if they want to take over. Ricci is excited to do so, but Joey isn't so sure. He's never wanted to be an owner, to take full responsibility for a business.

They assist at the bakery. Ricci learns the baking, books, and management, while Joey returns to deliveries. He uses his savings to buy another Buick that he drives from St. Anthony to Boulder, to Laforge, as far as Edmont and Broadview and Hexton. Joey meets a young woman, Nancy, while delivering to her parents' house, asks her out, and eventually marries her. When the Ricci parents and Joey's parents step down from the business, Joey tells the younger Ricci that he wants out. With his portion he puts a down payment on a ranch house for him and Nancy in a nearby town, Laforge.

Joey's father tells him that he knows a man named Vinnie, also Italian, who is opening a sausage factory in St. Anthony. Joey nabs a job. Vinnie gives him regular hours, a decent salary, benefits, and repetitive work. Joey is happy with all of it. Nancy continues delivering for Ricci's bakery into the early eighties, until it folds during the recession.

For Joey, the years when he and Nancy's son and daughter are growing up pass the quickest. There is always something to be done with or for them. Clothes-buying trips, baseball games, bike rides. Their high school plays against St. Anthony, where Ricci's sons attend. At games, Joey and Ricci stand next to each other, smoking and small-talking. Ricci dislikes working for someone else, but he does what he needs to do. Joey tells Ricci they should grab a beer, and they do, once or twice a year. Joey's and Nancy's son and daughter both go to Colorado State; they are the first in their family to attend college. Joey is proud of his kids, and glad that before his parents die, they are able to attend his kids' graduation. After college, his kids move to Wyoming. Colorado, they say, is becoming too populated.

The year their daughter, their younger child, graduates from college, Joey and Nancy find out that Nancy has ovarian cancer. They become familiar with hospitals and waiting rooms, with patient hospital staff and doctors who try to treat them as individuals but often come across as insincere because they've said the same thing to too many people too many times. By now, smoking is forbidden in most public spaces, so Joey goes to designated smoking areas or outside while Nancy waits for treatments or checkups. Her cancer is in remission three times, then comes back three times, over a span of fifteen years. Joey stops going out with work friends. His and Nancy's life becomes insular.

Joey wants to be the kind of person who becomes more gracious in suffering, not more bitter. But as the years go by, as the cancer returns, he can't help it. It's worse than Vietnam, he thinks once, when he had a date that his tour would end, when the daily expectancy of death would be over. He gets in fights with his boss, Vinnie, sometimes because the workers' wages have been flat. Vinnie says he has to cover rising healthcare costs. Joey likes Vinnie, who opens up the books and shows him. Joey hates himself when he becomes mad enough to yell. When Vinnie's son, Gus, starts working there, and pretends he's hot shit because his dad owns the place, Joey turns his anger on him. If Gus doesn't know the floor procedures, Joey yells them at him.

Vinnie dies right before the Great Recession. Gus takes over. After going over the books, Gus says he is doing away with health insurance. Four of the ten workers quit. Joey goes up to the office and yells at Gus. "Taking me off when we need it most," he says. "You're heartless." Gus promises to retain Joey's thirty bucks an hour, and says he should be able to buy health insurance with that.

Joey has to pay a third of his wages for a health plan that will cover Nancy's care. He wants a position with benefits. He finds the Riccis' home phone number in an old Rolodex. The younger Ricci, who still lives in the house, invites him over. When Joey stands on the porch, before he rings the bell, he imagines the hot summer nights when both families sat out there discussing the bakery. Ricci says to come on in. They stand in the entryway, then the living room. Ricci's own children are grown, he's divorced, and he's been dating someone for five years. As a manager at a restaurant, unlike the wait and kitchen staff, Ricci receives healthcare. Ricci says if he hears of a position with benefits, he'll let Joey know. They have little else to discuss except the past—the coal mines, the parades, the Italian community that has shrunk but is still there.

The last few months of Nancy's life, Joey smokes more. By the time she dies, one midnight in spring in hospice, he's smoking two packs a day. At the funeral, his kids try to convince him to move to Wyoming. He says he wants to live in his own house. Joey goes out even less now. He becomes the kind of person who always has the TV guide on the side table next to the recliner.

Five years after Nancy's death, Joey settles their medical debts through a reverse mortgage. By that time, Ricci has become the owner of a breakfast place in a strip mall. Every week, when Joey delivers factory sausage to Ricci's restaurant, they exchange greetings. An older lady, nicknamed "Honey," has started to work at the factory, and because her apartment is two blocks from Joey's house, he drives her to work. Every other Friday, when they're paid, he drives them both to the bank. He puts his own cash under his mattress as he used to as a delivery boy. He's living paycheck to paycheck.

Sometimes Joey lets Honey in his house for a smoke or a shot or to watch a game. One afternoon, while they're sitting at his kitchen table, she tells him she is Ricci's ex-girlfriend who he kicked out because of her drinking. Joey is surprised, then offended, then sad that Ricci hasn't mentioned that his ex is working at the factory. Another afternoon, she tells him that one of Ricci's sons lost his job and might not be able to pay rent. He goes to his room and gets cash from under his mattress and gives it to her. She acts surprised, but he thinks she hoped he'd do that. Every few weeks she complains, and every few weeks, he gives her money. She uses some of it for booze, he's sure, but he doesn't care.

That fall, for weeks Joey feels a mild ringing in his ears. By winter, he's throwing up. He knows it's lung cancer. He knows he won't go to a doctor. He's ready to die when his body wants to end. He doesn't want to linger like his wife. When his kids visit at Christmas and ask after his weight loss, he tells them he had pneumonia. That winter, his face pales and his coughing fits increase. He vomits once in the van when he's on deliveries. After that, he tells the restaurants that he's training another worker to take over deliveries for him, that he's thinking of retiring. Ricci says good for him, maybe they can get a beer sometime soon, and in the middle of the day, because he wants to retire, too. Joey asks Gus to let him work only two days a week, and he agrees. On his days off, Joey smokes nonstop on his couch, fading in and out of consciousness with the TV on. He can't remember when he stopped going out all together with Ricci—maybe when he was caring for Nancy? He knows it's his own fault he doesn't have friends at the end of his life.

One day he wakes up and can't move. When he can't feel his body or speak, he realizes he's died while asleep. When he doesn't pick up Honey for work, she walks over and lets herself in by the latched back gate, then the always-unlocked back door. She drops to her knees beside him, then calls 911, then Gus. She hangs up, sniffles, and tells him Gus has cancelled work for the day. Joey feels angry. To honor him they would work. Can't Gus even get that right? But immediately after, he doesn't care. He loves that he doesn't have to reply. He doesn't even have to look at her. When she goes into his bedroom and comes out with cash, he feels anger again, and again, it quickly fades. If she would've asked, he would have given it to her. His body cools. The stomach is the last warm spot, then the only sentient thing is his brain—or is it his soul? he wonders. His brain can't be functioning now.

There are over a hundred people at his funeral. Extended family, the Ricci family, and other family friends. Almost everyone from the factory. No outsider would know that he went days without seeing anyone. Ricci is crying. Joey feels tenderness toward him, and a sadness they won't talk again. Then he remembers they barely talked when Joey delivered to his restaurant. Even if Joey had lived longer, he wouldn't have had much to say to him.

On an overcast day, his son and daughter walk side by side, holding Joey's urn, on the bike path that wasn't there when he was a child, when he and the Ricci boys poked around this forest on foot until they found water. They stop where the creek opens into a beaver-dammed pool. When they spread his ashes into the creek, his consciousness will go too. After that, if he exists in any form, it won't be in this world. His daughter unscrews the lid and asks his son if he is ready. When his son nods, she begins to pour. Joey steels himself. He has said his goodbyes to the world, he knows, a long time ago. So long ago he can't even remember when.

# A DEAL

▰▰▰

I got the results from the paternity test and an offer for a new job on the same day. The paternity test was positive; I was the father. The new job was cutting meat at Chives, a specialty grocery store in Boulder. On my lunch break I texted my twin sister, Nicole, that I wanted to share two things with her on Skype. I told my coworker Lance the news after work at Fred's, our regular bar.

I was glad only we two had come out; none of our other coworkers were as discrete. He bought me a shot of whiskey to celebrate, and we settled into a game of pool with a pitcher of beer.

"You gonna fight for your rights with the kid?" he asked.

"I think so. If I can afford it."

"Good. Courts will be in her favor but you've got some things going for you."

Lance had a kid, not from a one-night stand, like me, but from a short-term marriage. He was upset he didn't have joint custody, but since he'd been on the road a lot when he worked as a train engineer, I thought the courts had decided correctly. Jodie, the mother of my child, was finishing her third year of med school and didn't know where she'd go for residency. I'd consider staying in town indefinitely, if the courts would look favorably on that.

Lance had two balls down to my one. I liked playing pool with him; we were both mediocre to fair. Some guys we worked with could clear the table before you drank half a pint. Lance dropped a third. He straightened and chalked his cue.

"I'd give you crap if I weren't leaving too," he said.

"Yeah?"

"More railway jobs have opened up. I should be gone by fall." He leaned over the table on one side, then moved to the other.

"That's great." He needed the money as much as I did, and he enjoyed being an engineer. I snapped my fingers. "Two of Gus's best, gone like that."

"Fuck Gus." He angled his pole too much and the ball bounced on impact.

I eyed the table. "Putting in my two-weeks tomorrow."

"Serves him right to lose his hardest worker. Son of a bitch."

I sunk a ball in a corner pocket. It felt good that Lance considered me the hardest worker. I thought of myself as the most reliable, but liked hearing it from someone else. I sunk two more before I screwed up.

"Did you like Laura when she was a baby?" I asked as he tried an off-the-wall shot. "I mean, kids are cool but I don't know about babies."

He laughed. "I liked her from the start. Not all dads do. Every year gets better. Not even worried about high school."

For me, having kids had always been something for the future. My sister had two. I refilled my beer. "Better when they can walk and talk. You can teach them stuff then."

"Laura liked soccer really young. Kicking a Nerf ball around."

I sipped until Lance knocked one of my balls in. I eventually won with one of his on the table.

"Good game," he said. "Another?"

"I have to meet Jodie."

"Oh Jesus. Good luck with that."

We exited the bar together. Usually, I'd take a left, toward County Road. From there I'd catch a bus to Laforge, where I rented a house with three others. Today I took a right with Lance toward Old Town St. Anthony.

"Where're you going?" he asked.

"Ernesto's."

"I hope she's paying."

"She said it's happy hour till seven."

"I bet."

It was a late April day, warm and windy, but I didn't trust it. Last winter, my first in Colorado, we'd had two six-inch snowfalls in May. I remembered telling Lance, a year ago February, while we broke and stacked cardboard boxes outside the shop in the snow, that I was glad winter was almost over. He'd stared at me. "We get most of our snow here in March and April," he'd said. Now, I unzipped my jacket and eyed the bare limbs. In Anderson County, West Virginia, where I was from, there'd be buds or leaves by now.

We raised our hands in goodbye as we split at the entrance to Ernesto's. It was a white stucco place with a Spanish-style roof. The inside was dimly lit and smelled like spaghetti. Waiters and waitresses dressed in black with white aprons floated by.

Standing in a corner, I glanced over black-and-white photos of coal mining St. Anth. Main Street with tall Western storefronts.

A boy in a coal cart. Two men with blackened faces holding picks. St. Anth and Laforge weren't so different historically from my hometown, except they had the resources—or the smarts—to move on from mining.

A menu on the wall detailed happy hour. The prices weren't bad; you could get a personal pizza for eight bucks. I didn't remember if I would've thought this cheap for a nicer restaurant in Anderson County. Probably not. Everything was more expensive here, the mountains larger, the women prettier. I'd thought my starting wage at the factory—ten per hour—pretty good, but after rent, food, and student loans, I didn't have much left. I'd worked up to fourteen an hour in two years, and at Chives I'd be making fifteen.

"Hey."

I turned to Jodie. She wore black slacks and a blue sweater, and was definitely starting to show.

"You kinda stink," she said.

I'd offered to go home and shower.

She stepped up to the hostess podium while running fingers through her dark hair. "Two for happy hour."

The hostess led us to a two-person table in the back. I sat where I could see the whole restaurant. She faced me, a hallway, and the wall.

"What rotation are you on now?" I asked.

She made eye contact with a passing waitress.

"So the test," I said.

"Food first."

She told the waitress we were ready while she poured our waters. I got the sausage, spinach, and feta pizza. Jodie ordered a house red, meatballs, fries, and some butternut-squash dish. She was animated and direct, qualities that attracted me the night we met, at Lunar, a bar closer to Main Street than Fred's.

I'd gone there only that once, and only because a bluegrass band was playing. I didn't even like bluegrass much: I just wanted to hear a sound from home. It was one of those fancy industrial-looking places, all exposed pipes and sleek counters, and she was at the bar. I sat two seats down. She laughed when I was visibly overwhelmed by the number of beers on tap.

"So the test," she said. She was sipping her wine.

She'd controlled the flow of conversation in the bar that night, and told me to kiss her thighs first thing in bed. But I wasn't a pushover.

"I'd like joint custody."

She looked amused. "I thought you'd say that. You're so responsible."

I'd suggested a condom that night. She said pulling out should be fine. Why did I agree? It was something in her demeanor, how she ran her hands casually over her breasts. Like she controlled the world, like she would not get pregnant unless she wanted to.

"I want to be part of his life."

"Are you sure you can afford it?"

"I got a new job."

She raised her eyebrows.

"At Chives. Comes with benefits."

"Moving up in the world."

I looked toward the front door. She was so classist. Why hadn't I noticed that? Maybe because at the bar I was busy telling her the story I always told to impress: that I was a computer genius at my rural high school, putting together motherboards at four-teen. That by the time I was a senior, the tech teacher paid me to fix electronics. That my parents cosigned on my loan to get a two-year tech degree at a college that shut down my final semester.

That night, she'd googled the school and said that students at a branch in Pennsylvania had filed a class-action lawsuit. "Not sure how it works across state lines but you might've been able to jump on that."

Our food came. We ate in silence. I liked the unique red sauce, the thin, crunchy crust. She was eating meatballs greedily. Through the front door, an older couple and a family arrived.

"I talked to my parents today," she said. She dabbed a napkin at her mouth. "We're prepared to buy you out."

"What?"

"What's left on your loan? Like, thirty thousand with the interest? We pay it off and you leave me"—she touched her sweatered stomach—"you leave us alone."

I chewed my last piece of pizza slowly, looking down. What kind of fucking deal was this?

She ordered another glass of wine. "You're a Colorado resident now, right? CU has a great computer-science program. You let us clear this debt, keep your Chives job, enroll in college too. By the time you're thirty you'll have a real degree and start earning real money. Or, by the time you're thirty, you can be sending money across the country for a four-year-old you rarely see, and between child support, loans, and whatever crap job you have you'll barely be getting by."

Our waitress brought Jodie wine and refilled my water.

"Is that even legal?" I asked.

"Why wouldn't it be?"

I gulped at the water. Her description of my future was not

far-fetched. Two of my coworkers had their wages garnished for kids they saw once a month.

"One minute," I said. I stood, turned, and headed down the hallway, where more black-and-white photos lined the walls. I glimpsed a small-town parade and kids at a drugstore counter before I pushed open the bathroom door.

In some ways she was offering me my dream. The life I could have had out of high school, if the school counselor had actually counseled me, if my parents, or myself, hadn't been so dumb. But to accept this life I'd have to pretend my son didn't exist. I didn't know if I could do that. I stared at my almost-clear piss before zipping up my jeans.

I looked straight ahead as I walked down the hall. At our table she was flushed and beautiful, pressing manicured fingers against her phone. I wanted our son to have her looks, my work ethic, and both our brains. For a moment I wanted to say that I'd follow her wherever she moved, that we could raise the kid together. But I knew she didn't want that, and besides these passing thoughts, neither did I.

She looked up. "We'll give you time to decide. Is a week enough?"

"Yes." I stayed standing.

She threw back the last of her wine.

"Is it OK to drink that?" I asked. My sister had stopped drinking while pregnant.

"Are you in med school?"

I put on my jacket.

"I'll get the check," she said.

"No." I pulled out my wallet and set down a ten.

I walked away while she was motioning for the waitress. Her confidence would stick with me, I thought. If I never saw her again, in ten years, long after I'd forgotten how we'd had sex, I'd remember how she could fetch a waitress with a simple head tilt and widening of eyes.

I passed the lights on Main Street in a daze. A lot of people were out enjoying the lapse in winter. But it had cooled since I'd entered the restaurant and was even cooler when I got off the bus. The breeze smelled like future rain.

At home, I went up to my bedroom, took off my clothes, folded them, and placed them by my bedroom door for morning. I took a quick shower, scrubbing off the sausage smell. I met Nicole on my desktop at eight.

"Hey!" She waved.

"Hey."

She was sitting at her kitchen table. Beside her were her waitressing nametag and a vase of lilacs.

"Mom says hello, too. Told her we were talking when she came to watch the kids."

"Hello to her too."

Nicole smiled, an outward smile, unlike Jodie, who smiled only to herself. She'd got the "best smile" in our high school yearbook, along with "most likely to marry her high school sweetheart." She didn't marry him, but she did marry her second serious boyfriend, Bryce, a salesman at a Honda dealership.

"Trevor wanted me to wake him but I said we'd talk to you during the day soon."

"I'd like that." Trevor was six. Rebekah, her other kid, was three. I remembered when Trevor had learned to walk, moving from knee to knee of us adults sitting on couch and chairs. I hadn't been around when Rebekah learned to walk. I hadn't been back since I'd left.

"Bryce's been showing him retro games. Maybe you guys could all play sometime over Skype."

"Sure."

She leaned forward. "What did you want to tell me?"

I rubbed my hands against my pajama pants. "I got a new job."

"Oh great!"

"Still cutting meat. But at a nicer place. And I get salary plus benefits."

"Awesome."

She was genuinely excited for me. I didn't know whether to be grateful or to tell her to raise her standards. My parents had taught us that a decent life required a good work ethic and avoiding debt. We'd internalized these values, and Nicole was happy. But what if she had unexpected medical bills? If Bryce died in a car accident? I doubted she'd know who to ask for advice any more than I did.

"And what's the other news?" Her eyes were sparkling, eager.

"Oh, well. I get to leave the factory," I lied.

She laughed. "That's great. That place sucks."

I ran a hand over my scruff and cleared my throat.

"But what's wrong?" she asked. "Your eyes look sad."

My damn eyes. I looked toward the white-washed wall. If I told Nicole, she'd advise me to fight for my rights. Concerning money, she'd say it would all work out. "Just tired," I said.

"You wanna get some sleep?"

I looked back at her. "You guys doing OK?"

"We're fine, Aaron. You sure *you're* OK?

"Yeah."

She looked like she wanted to reach through the screen and hug me. "I'm tired too," she said. "But let's talk soon. Maybe this weekend?"

"That sounds good. Love you."

"Love you too."

"Bye."

"Bye."

The screen went black. I retreated to my mattress on the floor. I leaned back, eyes closed. Outside, rain pattered against our plastic lawn table and chairs. I didn't mind. Rain was more forgiving than snow.

I shook off sleep and went to the unfinished basement, where a couple of my housemates liked to smoke pot. They were sitting on a dark green, frayed couch. The guy handed me a joint. The girl, a clerk at Chives, imitated problem customers, and we all laughed.

Two years ago, when I was overwhelmed by my loans and earning eight bucks an hour as a line cook, I'd almost illegally sold pot. I remembered the evening I got home from meeting with the supplier, sitting crisscross on my mattress, looking down, fingers interlaced against the back of my head. In high school I'd been voted "most likely to be the next Steve Jobs" and now I was reduced to this. I wanted to leave, to start over. I remembered the road trip my family had taken one summer to the Rockies. It was the most beautiful landscape I'd seen. I decided to go there. I knew my debt would follow me but I wanted to do something different.

And here was my real chance, I thought as my hit faded. I'd accept the offer. I didn't want more bills I couldn't pay.

Lance texted while I was in the kitchen making grilled cheese. She pay for the food?

Tried, I replied. Wouldn't let her.

Take from her all you can. You'll be paying a hell of a lot later.

I flipped the sandwich. I wouldn't tell Lance what she'd offered. In two weeks I'd be gone. He'd drift out of my life as all
coworkers eventually did. I'd go to college for computer science.
Maybe after I'd continue west, to Silicon Valley. I had the drive to
work there. Everyone in my family knew how to keep our heads
down. It was the connections we didn't have, the ability to ma-
neuver in complex bureaucratic or social situations.

I ate over the sink. Afterward, I went upstairs and lay on my
mattress listening to rain. I woke from a doze to my housemates
coming up the stairs. The downpour had stopped. Water dribbled in the gutters. I remembered the day. My son, who'd soon
be out in the world doing something apart from and unknown
to me. He was better off with her, I thought. If I raised him, he
wouldn't learn how to be savvy or ambitious. So far, I'd only
blindly worked hard.

The air felt humid. I stripped to boxers and cracked a window.
Maybe we'd skip the May snow this year, I thought. Maybe, if we
were lucky, the world would simply turn green.

# POKER NIGHT

◼◼◼

**M**onica had forgotten that she'd told Carlos he could have his coworkers over that night. After work, she'd bought a large pepperoni from their favorite pizza place, The Right Stuff. She'd imagined them eating while watching a movie, drinking only a couple beers, making love before or after they went to bed. But when she saw the cars curbside in front of her house, she remembered, and her gut hurt. Smoke rose over the back. They'd made a fire. On Fridays, they often got off work in the early afternoon, so they'd probably been drinking for hours. She lifted the pizza box and her purse and got out of the car.

In the kitchen, she ate a piece of pizza quickly. She didn't want the men to come inside and eat the whole thing before she had a chance to eat one slice. If she had a basement, she'd have sent them down there. The only other rooms in her house besides the kitchen were the living room, where you entered, and the bedroom and bathroom, in the back. If it hadn't been so cold outside, she'd have suggested they set up their poker game on the patio. As it stood, they'd have to play at the table at which she was eating.

She ate one more piece, then went out back with her coat on. As she approached the fire pit, Carlos turned his head and smiled. She scooted in next to him, and he petted her long hair.

Two guys across the fire were discussing whether they should play five-card or Texas hold 'em.

"You gonna play poker?" Carlos asked her.

"I don't know," she said. "Pretty tired."

He nodded toward a liquor bottle on the ground. "Take a swig. That'll wake you up."

"Or knock me out. I'll read for a bit. Join in later on."

"If you don't decide soon," Carlos said to the men. "I'll pick. It's my house."

"I think we've settled on five-card," one guy said. He reached a hand over the pit. "I'm Nathan. Have we met?"

"Monica." She shook his hand.

The others introduced themselves. She'd met Enrique, but not Aaron, Nathan, or Pete.

Enrique suggested they go inside, that it was getting too cold. Almost bare branches silhouetted against a darkening sky. The fire had fallen to embers. They'd burned an entire stump.

Inside, Monica sat on her bed reading the novel *Weaveworld* by Clive Barker. She'd taken up reading two decades ago while nursing her daughter Reina. It had helped pass the time all the years she was alone.

Monica was married for three years in her early twenties. She often thought that the only good thing to come from that was her daughter. After her husband left, she focused on caring for her: she saved up for a down payment, then for her education. Monica had run into Carlos in the deli line at King Soopers a year ago, right after Reina had graduated from Colorado State. Monica had admitted to herself that the timing of their meeting mattered as much as that it was him.

She'd had a crush on Carlos in high school. She'd liked how he'd rolled his compact body through hallway crowds, how he'd offered her a cigarette when she'd spotted him smoking behind the gym. At King Soopers, he was the one who'd spotted her, but by the time he mentioned them throwing pennies in the high school fountain, with his arm extended, his body reminiscent of its younger self, her attraction toward him had revived, and she invited him back to her house to share a meal.

The kitchen had quieted while Carlos was on a liquor run. Now, the game in process, Monica heard laughter, yells, and burps. She put her book aside.

In the kitchen, Aaron stood above the table, arms crossed. The other men sat playing.

She ran her eyes over the players, the pile of money.

"You know the rules?" Aaron asked.

Monica nodded, smiling. She'd been good at poker before she reached double digits. Her uncle had taught her to bet on hands with pennies.

"You out already?" she asked.

"I don't want to spend all I've got," he said. "You want a beer?"

He opened it for her, and they stood over the table, holding Coors Light bottles.

Monica's eyes flitted over hands of cards. She clucked to herself when a guy didn't risk enough on a good hand. Her desire for a quiet night with Carlos was fading, replaced with excitement for the game.

She'd finished the beer. "I think I'll play," she said.

"Take my seat," Nathan said. "I've lost enough."

She sat to the left of Carlos. A bottle of Jameson sat to his right. "Now you're in for it," Carlos said to the table.

They all anted up, and Enrique raised the bet. She had two kings and two jacks, and saw his raise. Enrique folded. Carlos went two more rounds, then she faced off with Pete. He had two tens and two queens.

"What did I tell you?" Carlos crowed as she pulled the money toward her.

Pete shrugged.

She won two out of the next five hands.

Pete shifted in his seat. "I'm low on cash," he said. "Can we bet alcohol?"

Carlos shook his almost-empty Jameson bottle. "I'd have to sit out."

"Of course you've drunk yours," Pete said.

"Like you didn't help."

"We could bet something else," Pete said.

"Maybe Nathan could cut off the loser's hair," Aaron said.

Carlos turned his head. "No one's cutting off my hair."

"Why Nathan?" Monica asked.

Enrique said he'd been trained as a barber.

"I don't have my clippers," Nathan said.

"I have some," she said.

Carlos turned to her. "You want your hair cut off?"

"Buzzes for the men, ear length for me." She smiled.

"How about it's just an option?" Nathan said. "Something you can bet on if you're out of money. Or just don't want to use it."

Carlos put his arm around her chair and grinned. "What the fuck," he said.

The other men said it was more or less OK with them. Nathan sat in to play another game. Pete anted up using money with the rest of them, then bet his hair on the second round. They all discussed whether he had to bet more money, or more hair, on the next round, but decided that by betting your hair you could stay in as long as you liked. Pete, who had a straight flush, won.

Pete won the next game too. Monica wondered whether he was going to bet his hair until he lost it. A couple games later, she had a full house. She considered folding to spare Pete the embarrassment, but then thought, at this rate, he was going to lose his hair sometime. Might as well be now.

Pete's face flushed when he lost.

"It's like he wanted to get his hair cut off," Aaron said.

Monica went to the bathroom to get her clippers and scissors. To save money, she'd cut Reina's hair. She'd trimmed Carlos's twice. He liked the longer, floppy look. On her way back to the table, she noticed that the Jameson was empty. Whether Carlos or the others had finished it, she didn't know.

Someone had pulled Pete's chair to the middle of the kitchen. He sat in it, elbows on knees, head in hands, rubbing his face.

"You need a haircut anyway," Nathan said. "Lots of split ends. I'm going to layer. One, two, three." He touched the bottom, middle, and top of Pete's head.

Pete nodded, and sat up.

Enrique went out back to smoke. Aaron grabbed another beer

from the fridge. Monica filled a glass of water and drank it over the sink.

"Indians look better with short hair anyway," Carlos said.

"Shut up," Pete said.

Monica turned. Carlos winked at her, and with a pack of smokes in hand, staggered out back. He had to grasp the door trim to steady himself.

Monica remembered her work holiday party last year, the first evening she admitted to herself that Carlos had a drinking problem. An open bar, and he was on his fourth or fifth while most nursed their first or second.

They'd discussed undocumented immigrants. Most people guardingly expressed their support, with glances in their direction, the only brown people there.

"Fuck illegals," Carlos had said. "Job snatchers."

The others said nothing. Some took a step back.

"You can't just let anyone in your country," Carlos continued. "Send them back."

"Most immigrants work hard," Monica said. "It's first or second generation, like us, who get lazy. Maybe they should send us back."

Carlos knocked his drink back and roared. "You might be onto something, sugar."

A drink or two later, after his speech became slurry, she suggested that they leave. She felt embarrassed, but also amused, that her date had caused a scene.

Every month or so, one of her coworkers would ask if she and Carlos were still together. When Monica said yes, the lady's face would sour. Monica felt defiant toward her coworker's disapproval, while also wondering whether she should be with him.

After Nathan finished the cut, Pete slipped him a couple dollars' tip. "I lost as fast as I could," he said. "Who wants to spend an hour's pay on a haircut?"

Monica laughed.

Over the next few deals, Monica bet her hair twice, but only when she was sure she'd win. As Carlos became more belligerent, it became more difficult for her to focus. For the most part the men ignored him. She felt relieved, but also sad, since this meant they were used to it. She wondered whether she should tell them all to leave, that the night was over, but she'd told Carlos they could stay as long as he liked. And she was enjoying the game.

She'd bet her hair on two aces and two queens. Pete was laying down his cards with hers, and she saw he had a royal flush.

"Someone needs a haircut," Pete said.

Carlos stood, knocking over the empty Jameson bottle with a hand thrust. "You're not touching her hair," he said.

"It's fine," she said. "I lost."

She hadn't had her hair short since high school, and although she hadn't planned on a cut, she was curious to see what it would look like.

Carlos got between her and Nathan. "I won't allow it."

"Maybe he could do it in her place," Aaron said.

Carlos raised his hand. "Yes."

"I lost. I'll do it," Monica said.

Carlos turned to her. "Your hair's so pretty."

"It'll grow back."

"It'll take a long time."

She wondered whether he'd be living at her place to see it. "If you want," she said.

Carlos grinned as he sat. "It's just a haircut," he said.

"It needs it anyway," Pete said.

Nathan laughed. "One, two, three," he said, showing Carlos the guards.

As Nathan cut, the other men formed a circle. No one went out back, as though they knew Carlos's haircut would be a spectacle. The whole room smelled like alcohol. Everyone else was drunk too; she hadn't noticed that. She was on the inside of the group, close to Carlos, and felt claustrophobic, as though the men were blocking her in.

Carlos's thick dark hair fell in chunks, then in shorter pieces, then in just wisps. He no longer smiled. He was grasping the seat of the chair, focused on not swaying.

"It's about time you did something for your girlfriend," Pete said. "Been mooching off her long enough."

Carlos stepped out of the chair and punched Pete in the jaw. His movement knocked off the clipper's guard, and the blade came down on his head. Pete stumbled back and caught himself on the table. Nathan yanked the clippers up and away. Carlos touched his head and looked at the blood on his hand.

Pete stepped forward and punched Carlos's cheekbone. Carlos staggered, straightened, then pulled a switchblade from his pocket and snapped it open. Monica drew in a breath.

"Ya basta," Enrique said.

Carlos glanced at him, then closed his eyes, putting a hand on his head. Enrique snatched the knife, snapped it closed, and told Pete to back up. Pete scowled and lowered his fists.

Carlos braced himself against the counter while Aaron pressed a kitchen towel against his head. Monica let out her breath and went to the bathroom for hydrogen peroxide and gauze. It could have been worse, she thought. She'd felt as though it was going to be for a second. By the time she returned, Aaron and Enrique were helping Carlos walk into the living room. They lowered him onto the area rug and he lay on his side. He blinked, not speaking, as though half unconscious, or startled, or in shock, or maybe just very drunk.

Monica kneeled next to him and dabbed the wound with peroxide. Every time the pressure touched a tender spot, he twitched, groaned, and rolled his eyes.

"I don't think it's that deep," Nathan said. "But it's hard to tell."

Pete was holding a sweating Coors against his cheek.

"Can you get me one," she asked. "Are they any left?"

Pete brought her one. Enrique got Carlos water. Monica helped Carlos sit up with his back against the recliner so he could hold the glass. "I think the game's over," she said.

The men got their things. She kneeled between Carlos's legs and examined his wound. More long than deep. She bandaged it while the men said their goodbyes and left.

She told him to stay awake in the recliner and monitored him in between tidying the kitchen, counting her money, and sipping at the beer. Almost three hundred dollars. She showed him her stash. Because he seemed more alert, she felt playful. "We could put it toward stitches if you need them."

Later, in bed, while sitting against the baseboard, she ran her fingers over his short, uneven cut. He lay flat on his back, awake, eyes closed.

"Your hair," he said. "Your hair's beautiful."

"Remember how short it was in high school?"

He was quiet for a while, then said, "Yes."

"Most girls wore it longer then. I think that's why I cut it. Something rebellious. It all culminated when I married that asshole Thad."

He rolled toward her. He always smiled when she called her ex "that asshole Thad." She was happy Carlos was the only man who'd lived with her in this house.

She scooted down and lay with her back to him. She wanted him to kiss her. She knew that with his injuries he should rest, and that even without them, he was probably too drunk to do much. "In high school, when we met, I felt closer to you than I'd felt to anyone in years," she said.

"I feel close to you too, sugar."

His voice was garbled. She didn't know if he'd remember any of this in the morning, and she didn't particularly care. Time had gone slowly while she was alone. When they were making love, or being quiet, or talking about nothing, it went fast, and she felt loved. She knew he wouldn't stop drinking. In a year or two, she wouldn't be able to handle it anymore, or maybe he'd tire of her sobriety, or maybe he'd do something so stupid that she'd kick him out. But for now, this was good. His breathing was even now, his face pressed against her neck.

She got up and filled glasses with water and set one on the floor on each side of the bed. If he woke dehydrated in the night, he could feel down there and find something to drink. She couldn't wait to see him, in whatever state he woke up. They'd have plenty of time for lovemaking in the morning.

# CHILDREARING

—•••—

O ne fall day, while cutting meat at the factory, Kathleen learned that her coworker Matt had gotten his girlfriend pregnant. Kathleen told him he'd made a mistake, and Matt said it usually was and it took two to party and what did she know about it? Kathleen moved the knife up and down, up and down again. She knew a little about it. She'd accidentally gotten pregnant while she and her husband, Jim, were engaged. She remembered fits of nausea while writing wedding invites. She told Matt he'd better be financially prepared to care for the baby, and he said, with his usual belligerence, that the law made him care for it whether or not he was prepared.

In the winter, Matt and his girlfriend moved in together, and based on Matt's stories, they were constantly bickering. His girlfriend wanted an abortion, then decided against it, then wanted one again when she was four months along, then because of Matt, or so he said, again decided against it. Kathleen went to a bar with the guys once to meet her. Her name was Erin, and she was a haughty girl, Kathleen thought. She didn't introduce herself and didn't make eye contact while Kathleen introduced herself. When Matt got loud while playing darts, Erin stared at him with open contempt. Granted, most people hated Matt, but Kathleen wondered how these two could live together.

Kathleen disliked that she called this young woman a *girl*, but she did, in her head, or over dinner with Jim, or gossiping with her daughter, Amy, when every month or so they drank whatever mixed drink was on special together at Old Chicago. Although her daughter still lived at home, Kathleen saw her less and less. Amy was working nights as a nurse and saving up for a down payment.

Amy tried to convince Kathleen to amp up her cake-making business, that it was a better fit for her than "whatever you do all day at the factory." Kathleen told her she liked the human inter-action, and Amy would say, "Yes, but *those* humans?" Her daugh-ter said she could hire an assistant for her business, but Kathleen knew she and Jim didn't have money for that. Kathleen loved small children, and thought she might work at a daycare center, if the ratio were two to one, children to adults. She didn't have energy to wrangle four to eight little ones.

In early April, Erin birthed the baby, a girl she named Taylor after Taylor Swift. Matt talked about Taylor nonstop, and cut meat slower, and Gus, the boss, yelled at him at least once a day. Kathleen thought it unfair that Gus picked on him since almost everyone was cutting slower: in the warming weather, no one wanted to be in a factory that felt like an icebox.

Sometimes Kathleen stood for minutes watching the knives of other workers. When she was younger, she was an efficient waitress. As a receptionist at a dentist's office, she promptly filed insurance claims, printed out invoices and mailed them. But now she felt unmotivated and didn't care. She wasn't paid for raising Amy. Now she was paid for not working much; in her calculations, just catching up.

"Can you take out the boxes?" Gus said one day as she zoned out. He might have yelled at her if she hadn't known him since high school, when he used to play drums in a local rock band, before he was so bitter. For some reason, this cowed him.

She nodded and took off her gloves. She broke down the boxes with a box cutter and carried them outside and toward the dumpster. On her right was a row of their cars, Matt's red Escape on the end. The windows were halfway down, and she heard squawking. She dropped the boxes, rushed over, reached over the window, and unlocked the door. In the backseat, a baby squirmed in a small, foldout crib. She raised her up and out and to her chest.

"I was just about to check on her," Matt said from behind.

She turned. She remembered he'd already taken two smoke breaks. She didn't know whether she was more surprised that Taylor was here or that Matt had been able to keep it a secret. "This an everyday thing?" she asked.

"Hell no. Taylor has the sniffles. Erin's trying to take the day off. Should be here any minute."

It was an insane setup, Kathleen thought, even negligent. The baby fussed, moving against her chest. "You have a bottle or something?"

Matt stuck his head and arms in the truck and came out with a bottle. "She likes it better warm but she'll drink it." He held his arms out for Taylor. Kathleen took the bottle.

Matt made a face at something behind Kathleen. She turned to Gus.

"What the hell," he said. "I should fire you both."

"We'll be in in a minute," Kathleen said.

Gus muttered, but turned and went inside. Kathleen fed Taylor, marveling at her tiny nose and fingers, then stayed outside with Matt and the baby until Erin pulled up a few minutes later.

Over dinner, Kathleen and Jim reminisced about the hectic period of shuttling Amy between family and daycare providers. They'd both had full-time jobs for their first seven years of parenting. After that, Jim received a promotion, and Kathleen had stayed home. She liked running the household, and Jim was happy to let her run it. When Amy was in fifth grade, Kathleen started to dabble in baking for profit. A few years ago, with their retirement on the horizon, she'd decided to get a steadier job.

In late summer, over sack lunches in the break room, Matt told Kathleen that the daycare Erin worked at no longer allowed her to take the baby with her.

"I never understood why they allowed her to begin with," Kathleen said. "I'd never heard of a place doing that."

"They had an inspection to renew their license or something. They're supposed to be a toddler and preschool daycare, not infants."

Matt was talking while he chewed.

"What are you going to do now?" Kathleen asked.

"Erin's mom will take her Tuesdays and Thursdays. Sucks cause she's all the way in Edmont. You want to watch her the other days?"

Kathleen was so surprised she spoke with her mouth full. "And, what, quit here?"

"Gus would let you work a couple days a week."

"I doubt it."

"You could ask."

"Maybe I will." She didn't really like Matt, but she didn't want to immediately shoot down a request from an anxious new father either.

That afternoon, she and Amy watched *House* together. They were on season six. Amy looked over at Kathleen with those big brown eyes that hadn't changed much since she was a baby, and asked why she wasn't making her usual snide comments. Kathleen shrugged but after Amy left for work she mentioned the idea to Jim. She said she wouldn't mind being away from the factory a few days a week, as long as Matt paid her. Jim said that sounded just fine, so the next morning Kathleen went upstairs and asked Gus, while the others unloaded tubs of meat from the walk-in.

"Do whatever you want," he said.

"OK, I'll just be working Tuesday and Thursday then," she said.

She hadn't planned to make the decision then. It was something about Gus's noncommittal poise, how she felt he couldn't care less.

She and Matt decided he'd pay her ten dollars an hour under the table. Anything more and there wouldn't be much point for him and Erin both to work. It was four dollars less per hour than her current pay, but she wouldn't pay taxes on it, and even though she slacked at the factory, her body would appreciate a rest from all that.

Not that caring for a six-month-old wasn't labor intensive—but fewer repetitive motions were involved, and Kathleen decided her routine. After getting up at 5 for the past four years, it was relaxing to wake up at 7 or 8 three days a week, to not feel exhausted every morning.

Erin dropped off Taylor at 8:45, right before the baby's first nap. After Kathleen gave her a bottle and put her down, she'd pore over her cookbooks and websites for recipes, bookmarking ones she wanted to try. In between Taylor's naps, she'd take her on a walk in her stroller, then read or sing to her. During Taylor's second nap, Kathleen would bake. Matt would pick Taylor up at 2:30 or 3, arriving as the baby woke. Kathleen was amazed that he showed up sober, and even asked him about it.

"Tuesdays and Thursdays are my drinking days now," he said. And she felt proud of him, that he'd made this change.

If the baby cried, Amy, who slept during the day, complained.

"I don't know what to say," Kathleen said. "She cries less than any baby I've ever known."

"You just say that because she's your surrogate grandkid."

Amy had found a condo in Hexton, which was closing within weeks. She and Kathleen's conversations often had this edge now, as though nothing was permanent. Every afternoon, when Amy woke up, instead of watching TV with Kathleen, she'd carry another something out the door for Goodwill.

"You won't have anything to put in that place," Kathleen said one day.

"I don't want old stuff. I want new stuff," Amy replied. She held a lamp—it had been Jim's mother's, Kathleen remembered.

"Why don't you leave that one here?" Kathleen said. "They don't make lamps like that anymore."

Amy set down the heavy brass lamp in the middle of the sitting room. The shade was yellowed with age. "There you go," she said and headed down the hall for something else, Kathleen thought. Something else to give away.

One afternoon when Matt came to pick up Taylor, Kathleen asked him what they were doing for Thanksgiving.

"I was going to make a turkey and that's it," Matt said.

"Why don't you cook the turkey and bring it here?" Kathleen asked. "We have plenty of sides. I often run out of meat, I have so much family."

Matt looked around the kitchen and sitting room, as though it were filled with people. "We won't know anyone."

"You won't be the only ones. Always some new boyfriend or girlfriend stopping by."

On Thanksgiving, when Kathleen opened the door to them, she thought of the holy family at their first extended get-together back from Bethlehem. Erin was ten years younger than Matt, and defiant, as Mary would be, after having a child "out of wedlock" and everyone talking. Matt, who wore a black stocking cap, held the turkey in a pan covered with foil. Behind them it was snowing. "The turkey might be a little dry," Matt said. "Erin forgot to check on it."

"We were both supposed to check on it," Erin said. She was holding Taylor, who was wearing an orange onesie.

In the kitchen, Kathleen took the turkey and served them each a mug of hot cider. Kathleen's extended family had already arrived. She gathered everyone around the table to pray, then they served themselves buffet style and ate while standing or sitting around the open sitting and dining rooms. Erin sat on the couch above Taylor, who sat on the carpet near Kathleen's eighteen-month-old great-niece. Kathleen was pleased to see that Taylor could now pass colored blocks from one hand to another. Matt stood behind the couch, his arms crossed against his chest, his dirty-blond hair flattened from the cap, chatting with Amy. Amy asked a question, as usual her hands speaking before her voice. Kathleen imagined them as siblings, and wondered how different her life would have been if she and Jim had had another kid. At the beginning of their marriage, money was too tight, and they'd only halfheartedly tried again for a couple years in their mid-thirties. In that scenario, Amy would be the older, and their younger one would be around Erin's age, and probably still living at home. Amy had moved out in mid-October.

Matt and two of Kathleen's nephews took their dessert and spiked cider into the kitchen and started talking politics. Others stayed in the sitting room, watching football. Kathleen bobbed around, refilling coffee or cider or milk, then sat on the couch. Amy scooted over and leaned her head on Kathleen's shoulder, as she used to as a child. Amy had become more childlike toward her since she moved out; maybe, as an adult living in her child-hood home, she'd had to establish herself, but now that she had her own place, she could revert to childishness without losing self-respect. Kathleen took Amy's hand and held it.

"Matt's a character," Amy said.

"What did he say now?"

"He just says whatever comes to his head. I'm not sure if he's a loud mouth or awkward."

Kathleen laughed. "That's a good way to put it." She nodded

toward Erin, who sat in a recliner feeding Taylor a bottle before her nap. "Taylor's pretty cute, you think?"

Amy tensed so Kathleen knew not to go there, though Kathleen wasn't sure whether she was insinuating that Amy should have kids or simply admiring Taylor. As Kathleen's eyes turned toward the TV, Amy's body relaxed.

When Kathleen heard Taylor on the monitor waking up from her afternoon nap, Erin was dozing, so Kathleen stood. She and Matt stepped down the hall at the same time. "I got her," he said. "You're good, I got her."

"It's OK," Kathleen said. "Go enjoy yourself." From his loudness, Kathleen could tell he was tipsy. Erin hadn't been drinking, so maybe they'd arranged she would drive.

Matt shouldered his way in front of Kathleen and into the small spare room, where Kathleen had moved junk to the side to set up a crib. Taylor lay on her back, fussing. Matt lifted her halfway out, then lost his grip and dropped her. Kathleen stepped forward in time to see Taylor's head bounce against the bottom of the crib. She sucked in her breath as Taylor cried louder.

"Let me get her," Kathleen said.

"I got her."

"Maybe you could warm up some milk?"

"I don't want you to watch her if you're going to try to take over."

Kathleen felt the words as a pain in her chest. She wanted to continue to watch Taylor, and she wanted to be able to trust Matt with his own child. She made a point not to speak as Matt scooped her up and sat in the rocker, his face very red, Taylor growing louder. When Erin stepped in the room, Matt asked her to warm a bottle. She looked between him and Kathleen before she nodded and stepped out. "I'm good," Matt said to Kathleen. Taylor was still screeching.

"Don't you think you should check her head?" Kathleen asked.

"I'm good," Matt said again, not looking at Kathleen, though he moved his hand to more firmly cup Taylor's head.

"OK," Kathleen said, and left.

In December, Amy had a housewarming party. Kathleen thought her daughter's style too sparse and modern, but the new furnishings inspired her to look into doing what she could do, on her and Jim's budget, to freshen up their own place. They still missed Amy, but it was nice to have Taylor around. She pulled herself to her feet for the first time in January, while Kathleen was babysitting her, and in February, she began walking, at less than eleven months. Kathleen bragged to everyone in the factory, and made Amy come over just to see it. Sometimes when Taylor toppled over, she'd cry out "Dee," the same nickname the baby Amy had called Kathleen.

On the first Monday in March, Matt knocked early. Kathleen, who didn't want the noise to wake Taylor, set her cake-battered spatula in the bowl and hurried to the door.

He stood on the doorstep, looking down, hands in pockets. "I quit," he said.

She invited him in.

He looked at the beige carpet as he walked through the sitting room. She motioned toward the table. "I'll make you a drink. How about milk and brandy? I put honey and cloves in it."

He nodded. They were silent as she warmed the milk. After

she set the drink in front of him, she went back to putting batter in cake tins.

"All my twenties I worked so many different jobs," he said. "I just wanted to work at one place forever. And how long did I make it? Six years."

He was not in a mood for her to say that the factory was not the best place to work at forever, Kathleen thought. "Worked there longer than most people," she said.

He cupped his hands around the warm mug. "I wanted to know when I woke up what I was doing every day. I just wanted that."

His face flushed. She thought he might cry.

"You want something to eat?" she asked.

He shook his head. He gulped air until the threat of crying had passed. He breathed hard, then took a sip.

Kathleen put the cake pans in the oven. She rinsed out the mixing bowl and put it in the dishwasher. She came to the table and sat across from Matt. "I'm sorry," she said.

He pursed his lips. He took another sip and held up the glass. "Thanks. For the drink. For taking care of Taylor."

"Don't worry about it," she said.

The baby began to fuss on the monitor. Kathleen rose. "I got her," Matt said.

By the time Matt returned, Kathleen had warmed a bottle. She handed it to Matt and he sat back down to feed her. The little girl took the bottle from Matt's hands to hold it herself. "My dad used to mix brandy with milk in my bottle," Matt said. "Not that I'm much better," he said.

"I remember tasting beer at three or four," Kathleen said. "Sitting on our porch in Old Town St. Anth."

"No shit."

Kathleen took a Tupperware container from the fridge and put it in Taylor's paisley-orange diaper bag. "You're better," she said. "You're a good dad."

Matt plucked a cloth from the bag and wiped milk off Taylor's mouth. "I think I'm gonna stay home with her," he said.

Kathleen raised her eyebrows.

"Until I find another job. I want to take my time to find a good one this time. Like maybe with the city. Trimming trees or something."

Kathleen nodded. "Will Erin be OK with that?"

Matt's face tightened, then relaxed. "I think so. I mean, I'll end up with a better job. Eventually. I hope."

Matt stood, Taylor in his arms, and threw the bag over a shoulder.

"This is it, then?" Kathleen said.

"Yeah I guess. I owe you for today."

"Oh don't worry about that."

"I owe you for more than that."

"I'm sure I'll see you soon." She kissed Taylor's cheek, then opened the door for them. It was snowy outside, maybe icy. "You OK to drive?" she asked.

He nodded and smiled. Taylor obliviously waved goodbye.

Kathleen sat at the table and drank the rest of Matt's drink. It was so sudden, Taylor being gone for good. It was difficult to wrap her mind around it. After the timer rang, she took out the cake tins. It was a simple vanilla two-layer cake, and while it cooled, she made a chocolate frosting with melted chunks of baking chocolate, softened butter, milk, and powdered sugar.

While she lathered on frosting, she decided she'd take the cake to the factory tomorrow. She'd feed everyone, including Gus, then ask for her full-time job back. He couldn't say no, now that Matt had left. Or maybe he couldn't say no to her.

It was three o'clock. Neither Taylor nor Amy would be waking up from sleep. For a minute, Kathleen stood at the kitchen counter, listening to the silence. Then she went into the sitting room, sat on the couch, and searched for something to watch on daytime TV.

# MURALS

●━●━●

Cynthia finished the mural in downtown Boulder the day before Easter, one she'd been commissioned to do soon after Lance had left town. She still had reservations about painting it—a mural that depicted different races with clasped hands side by side in a town where many brown people lived in the small apartments she'd grown up in and many white people in nicer apartments or houses—but she enjoyed painting and the building's owner was paying her twenty dollars per square foot. At least she wouldn't have to see it every day: she'd moved to the more Latino Laforge seven years ago after her mom died, and these days she went through Boulder only to go on a hike with her older brother Eddie or to visit him at his condo in Nederland, one of the towns toward the mountains. Both of them were working during the day on Easter, she as a bartender, he as an EMT, but they planned to meet up in the evening.

At home—a five-hundred-square-foot one-bedroom apartment on the second story of an old white stucco house divided into four units—she took a bath. The muscles in her shoulders, arms, and back had been strained from painting the mural, more than she thought they would be, since she painted canvases regularly in her apartment, and had even muraled most of her bedroom. She'd lived there five years, and the landlord, who rarely entered her unit, never entered her bedroom, so a couple years ago, she'd pencil-sketched along the white walls, then eventually painted three out of four of them. The apartment complex she'd grown up in, her mom, her brother, some friends, her high school soccer fields, the coffee shop where she'd worked from ages eighteen to twenty-two, the Laforge bungalow she'd rented with a few friends, this stucco house, the long counter at the bar in St. Anthony, where she worked now, guys sitting on stools, their backs to the viewer. She'd thought she'd maybe paint Lance facing out but was now glad she hadn't. She'd whitewash the mural before she moved out, but that would be a while: she didn't know where else she'd find a pet-friendly place with cheap rent and such an inattentive landlord.

She was curled up on her navy-blue couch watching episodes of *It's Always Sunny* and petting her large black dog, Meadow, when Lance texted. Great sunset today, was all he said, with a photo of a deep orange ball of sun lowering behind a flat, snowy landscape. Very pretty, she texted back, then sent him a photo of the Boulder mural. Finished today! she wrote. Very nice! he texted. But I still like the one in your bedroom better. She wasn't sure whether this comment was sincere or hinted toward their intimacy. Probably both. She liked the one in her bedroom better too. But the instructions said to paint people of different races holding hands. She'd decided the figures would hold their hands above their heads. This choice improved it but she still thought it would look better on the side of an elementary school, not the side of a business.

All the Easter regulars were there the next day, except for an older guy, Joey, who'd died last summer. Lance and his former coworkers from the factory had worked closely with Joey. Some had more fondness for him than others, but all of them openly mourned him for weeks afterward. They'd sit at the large round table or play darts while telling stories of how he stood up to their boss, or how he'd drink food out of a straw because he didn't have teeth, or how he'd refused cancer treatment. She herself remembered him as a gruff man who visited Fred's only on Easter, and would tell her which buildings used to house which businesses in Old Town St. Anth if asked. Today, the regulars left his stool empty. She placed his drink, a martini, on the bar counter as a memorial, then went about her business.

By lunchtime, Billy wanted to talk about Easter. "It's the most important holiday for Christians," he said. "Don't know what the fuss about Christmas is all about." His bushy gray eyebrows had a mind of their own. Cynthia agreed while she got him another rum and coke. "Everyone is born," Billy said. "That didn't prove his deity. He proved his deity by coming back to life."

Again, she agreed. She listened to him proclaim Christ's deity every Easter like some bar priest. As she washed glasses, she scrunched her face at the thought of Eddie's fiancée, Isabel, who was probably at an Easter mass right now, and would probably accompany Eddie later. Cynthia found Isabel boring: she had her mother's nurturing nature and obsession with religion without her grit or capacity for delight. Isabel was always talking about wanting babies and the meals she cooked, traditional gender roles that sounded constricting to Cynthia, which was probably why she gravitated toward middle-aged men who led peripatetic lives, like Lance, who was thirty-eight and a train engineer. She'd also been involved with, among others, a guy who frequented Hong Kong on business trips and a guy whose immediate family lived in the Czech Republic.

"You go to church today, Billy?" Cynthia asked as she heard him telling Jasmine, another Easter regular, about the women who found Jesus's tomb empty.

Billy straightened up. "I know everything taught there. What's the point? You all need to hear it here."

Cynthia exchanged looks with Jasmine, then they both laughed.

"What's so funny?" Billy asked.

"I been hearing that story my whole life," Jasmine said. "Cynthia too, I think."

"You'd be surprised who doesn't know it," Billy said. "And there's a difference between knowing and understanding," he added.

Cynthia thought he looked as pitiful as Meadow right before she left for a work shift. "You're right," she said. "You never know who knows and doesn't know, Billy."

His face relaxed into a smile, then he took his drink to the foosball table.

"How you doing?" Jasmine asked Cynthia.

"I'm good." Cynthia poured Jasmine a glass of chardonnay. "How about you?"

"Happy to be here. By the time I return from my 'walk,' my girls should be glazing the ham." Jasmine was one of the few who didn't come to the bar on Easter because she lived alone but because she wanted a break from her family. "You doing anything after work?"

"Meeting my brother at Rodrigo's."

The mural Cynthia had finished was on the building across from the restaurant, and although she was ambivalent about the content, she was sure about the quality, and wanted Eddie to see it.

Jasmine nodded toward the martini. "For Joey?"

"Yes."

"Heard but not till after the funeral."

"The sausage boys keep me informed."

"You still going with that one . . . ?"

"Lance. Not really."

Jasmine looked past Cynthia. "*Not really.* I know how that is."

Cynthia wondered why she hadn't said no, then thought probably because she wasn't involved with anyone else yet. She was getting older, and was not as nimble or proactive in picking up guys. She smiled to herself at the half-true thought while cutting lemons and limes.

Jasmine wanted to hug Cynthia before she left, and Cynthia let her because she liked her, though she didn't usually hug customers. A regular couple arrived, and Cynthia played a game of darts with them. She was better at pool than darts, but had improved her dart game lately, since a new bartender liked to play as she was leaving, when he was taking over. Billy became drunker as the afternoon progressed, but not violently so; he crooned Easter hymns to himself at the round table in between proselytizing and foosball.

A few minutes before six, when her shift would end, Cynthia turned to see Lance sitting next to Joey's old seat, his large shoulders hunched, his face a full smile. She took a step back. His presence was so different from the thought of him.

"Joey's drink." He nodded at the martini.

"It's a memorial. Been there all day. Probably got my spit in it." She grabbed the glass, turned, and tossed the liquid in the sink.

"Hello to you too," he said.

She turned back and smiled. "Hello. You surprised me. That was your plan?"

He nodded. His smiled had faded. His eyes were earnest. She leaned over to touch the indent in his chin, then went to get him a whiskey neat. "Just a single please," he said.

She poured it, then set it in front of him. "Drinking less?"

"I don't have to cope from working at that place. It's nice to be on the road again." He sipped the whiskey. "Though nothing beats our trip to Grand Junction."

In December, they'd gone on a train trip through the Rockies to celebrate him landing his job. In a canyon, trestles held up tracks a hundred feet off the ground. Cynthia loved looking down into the depths, then up at the peaks.

She turned to Toby, her replacement, who was asking a question about food prep. She answered, then introduced him to Lance. "Lance was a regular here for a couple years," she said.

"Nice to meet you, man," Toby said. "You have time for a game?" he asked Cynthia.

"A quick one," she said. "I'm meeting my brother for dinner."

Lance's shoulders slouched more. "We already had plans," Cynthia said.

"Maybe we could meet up later?" he asked.

"I don't know how long I'll be out. I'll keep you posted."

He nodded.

"You want to play darts?" she asked.

He finished his whiskey and stood.

She learned over the game that he'd already seen his ex and middle-school-aged daughter. "Saved the best for last," she said.

"Always," he said. "You're better at darts now."

"Things change," she said.

He could have looked her up on his earlier leaves that winter, but didn't, which Cynthia didn't mind. She wouldn't have been ready to see him then, but she was ready now. He leaned his whole long upper body too far forward as he shot, not good form but endearing. After the game, they kissed lightly outside the bar before Cynthia rode the bus home to walk Meadow. On the ride, she smiled at Lance's childlike delight at Joey's drink, at the darts. When relaxed, he was good company. She was glad he hadn't lost interest in her.

As Cynthia leashed up Meadow, she told her she had to leave again soon, but that they'd spend the whole next day together. They walked by refurnished mining shacks, Cynthia's regular laundromat, the local theater. On Main Street, a regular cashier nodded to Cynthia from inside a Latino corner grocery store, and Cynthia nodded back. She thought of Eddie, of how he wanted her to leave the service industry. Because she loved and respected him, because he was her closest living family member, she always listened to his advice, though she knew his wants and desires would never align with hers. Once, about a year ago, during their first conversation on the topic where she'd resolved not to argue, he'd even suggested that she might have been more traditionally ambitious if, like him, she'd remembered emigrating from Guadalajara. He'd been only three (and their mom pregnant with her), so she doubted he remembered it as much as he claimed. "I like that my job gives me the headspace to paint in my off hours," was all she said. "You could still paint while having a better job," he'd said. "You can't live like this forever."

Her watercolor landscapes being featured in an art walk last summer and her being commissioned to do the mural this winter had given her more confidence that she could in fact live like this forever. And maybe Lance would be a good long-term match for her, she thought as Meadow gulped from the water bowl outside the ice cream shop. Cynthia liked his body, his optimism, his hardworking nature. And his desire to be on the road also attracted her, and he was on the road a lot now, so even if they became an official couple, she'd have weeks at a time to be by herself and paint. As she walked by a flea market and back into the neighborhood, she pulled out her phone. I want to see you later, she wrote. If you want to go over early and let Meadow out, she'd like that. She's had a long day alone, she added in a second text.

Great! he replied. I'll head over in about an hour. Watching a game with Aaron.

Cynthia took a quick shower, then set Meadow up on the couch with a rawhide chew and told her Lance would be over to play with her. Meadow banged her tail as though she understood; she liked it when Lance came over.

Eddie and Isabel were on the open-air roof deck of the restaurant, sitting at a table with their backs to the mural, jars of margaritas in front of them. Cynthia sat across from them, facing her painting. They exchanged greetings, then anecdotes about their days. Isabel had been to mass with her extended family, as Cynthia had expected, and Eddie, like Cynthia, had had a quiet shift. "People don't get as suicidal at Easter as Christmas," he said.

After they ordered food, Cynthia mentioned the mural, pointing behind Eddie and Isabel so they'd turn their heads. Another group who'd just arrived blocked the view. "We might need to stand," she said. They all walked to the railing.

"Whoa," Eddie said. "It's the largest painting you've done, right?" He'd seen her bedroom mural, and a few of her acrylic, oil, and watercolor paintings, but he'd been working during the walk that had featured her art.

"Yes."

"I love it," Isabel said.

Cynthia liked the simplicity of the painting even less.

"I like what you have," Eddie said. "But are you done? That empty area behind it."

"I thought I was done, yes," Cynthia said.

The empty space bothered Cynthia as she ate. "Maybe it's not done," she said.

"What?" Eddie asked. He'd been snatching beans off Isabel's plate, while she slapped his arm lovingly.

"The mural," she said.

"I do like the busyness of the one in your bedroom better," Eddie said.

"That's what Lance said."

Eddie became solemn. "You still talking to that guy?"

"Off and on. He's on the road for his railway job mostly."

"You be careful."

He said that about every white guy she was interested in. She changed the conversation to Eddie and Isabel's upcoming September wedding, a topic she knew Isabel would latch on to. They'd decided to have a ceremony at her church, Isabel said, then a reception in the mountains.

"You could add mountains to the background," Eddie said, and glanced over his shoulder. "You're good at painting those." The customers who had blocked the view of the mural were gone; Cynthia could see the raised arms and clasped hands but not the faces.

"I like it how it is," Isabel said. "Friendly. Clear."

"Mountains, OK, maybe," Cynthia said. "Maybe apartments too. Like the ones we grew up in. And some Boulder houses."

Isabel jutted out a bottom lip.

"That sounds good," Eddie said.

"You could add churches too," Isabel said. "One Catholic, one Protestant."

"I like that idea," Cynthia said, surprising herself. "I'll start right after this."

After Isabel took off to her sister's place, Cynthia showed Eddie the closet where she stored the lights, ladder, smock, paint, brushes, and tins. She set up the floodlights across the alley, facing the side of the building. It was dark outside the light's beams, but she preferred to work at night with fewer people gawking or just around. She was thankful Lance was with Meadow so she didn't feel rushed to get home. She was also happy to be alone with her brother.

"Do you ever get scared being alone out late at night?" he asked.

"No." She waited for him to tell her to be careful but he didn't. After she sketched some apartments in her notebook, he handed her the colors she asked for so she wouldn't have to get off the ladder. It was a much faster way to work than alone. "You could be my assistant," she joked.

"I think my job pays a bit more per hour."

He stayed until she'd finished painting the apartments and had sketched a brick church.

"It's getting there," he said, looking over her shoulder.

"I'm glad you approve." She smiled. "Almost hiking season." It was something Isabel hated, hiking.

"I want to show you this lake I found in October."

"OK."

"Maybe I'll bring Miguel?"

He was always trying to set her up with some nice Mexican guy. Since high school, in fact.

"OK," she said.

"You don't give a fuck about him, do you?"

"No I don't."

They both laughed.

She gave him a goodbye hug, then checked her phone. Just a photo of Meadow asleep half on top of Lance on the couch.

Who needs me when Meadow is there? she texted back.

Any ETA? he asked.

She looked up at the mural. Lots to do but the bus ran only till midnight. Twelve, she replied.

We'll be here napping, he wrote.

She sketched a racially ambiguous Jesus onto the door of the church, and thought Billy, and probably Jasmine too, would be pleased. She sketched a Victorian and large modern-style Boulder house and behind them aspens and mountain peaks. She started to paint, but it took longer to bring the equipment up the ladder without an assistant, and the evening was getting on, so she quit. The building's owner had requested it finished by June 1, so she had time, and it also felt good to know there was more painting to be done. It gave her something to look forward to.

While she waited for a bus, a feeling of pleasure rose in her muscles. In anticipation of sex, yes, but also pleasure in the soreness from where the work had entered her body. Unlike yesterday, the pain was not acute but more of a memory, muted. It was growing chillier outside but she'd brought her jean jacket for that.

After she put it on, she checked her phone. That canyon our train went over might look good on your empty bedroom wall, Lance had written. What do you think?

She envisioned the painting, from sky and peaks to train and trestles to the Colorado River. It would be a nice contrast to the more everyday scenes on the other walls. I love that idea, she thought, then texted.

# AT THE LAKE

●–●–●

R ick left in early September, when it was still hot outside, before the leaves in the lower elevations of the Front Range started changing color. Meryl had known he was going to leave for almost six months, but the quietness of the house still surprised her. She didn't hear him showering upstairs while her Earl Grey steeped; she didn't hear him in the spare room on the treadmill while she was making dinner. And no one accompanied her on her evening walks around the lake. In the mornings once a week or so a girl friend would walk with her.

Their house and its proximity to the lake were some of the reasons Meryl didn't want to retire to a complex in Sun City, Arizona. They'd lived in the house since the late eighties; she'd finished raising three children next to the lake and watched its playgrounds improve, and more recently, the City of Laforge had set up a Frisbee golf course. "If it was real golf, I'd consider staying," Rick had said, even though he frequented a golf course only a couple miles from them. She knew the real reasons for his desire to leave: he wanted to play golf year-round and since his layoff the area had reminded him of his supposed failure. Four years ago, soon after a media conglomerate bought out the independent publisher where Rick had worked IT for twenty-nine years, he was fired. It was then he'd begun discussing moving full-time to Sun City; before that, they'd planned to go there in their retirement for only one month during the winters. As he became more adamant about leaving, she became more determined to stay. And so they'd agreed to separate, though they'd put off a divorce.

Two weeks after Rick left, Meryl harvested the remaining green tomatoes from her large side-yard garden. She made a casserole with some, and with others, placed them in paper bags, then in the basement to ripen. The casserole was too large for one person, so she brought the leftovers to the break room at the library. Meryl had thought that after Rick left she'd become more social at work, but at least in these early days after his departure, she chatted less. Her coworkers sounded like Rick: Why didn't she leave with him? What was she doing at sixty-six still working? But she hadn't received her MLS degree until her youngest was in high school, and she wanted to work as a librarian until she could collect her full social security. She thought Rick, who had wanted to work until at least age sixty-seven, too, should have understood this desire, even if her coworkers didn't. In another year, if the library wanted to force her out for someone younger, fine. She didn't know what would fill her days in retirement, but she'd figure it out, as she'd figure out how to live without Rick one day, one season at a time.

Laforge had a Halloween snowstorm that year, the drifts covering Meryl's dying tomato vines, but the region didn't receive sustained snow until early December, when Rick texted her photos of him-self golfing while she was ordering Nordstrom and Macy sweaters online. And what would have happened to her drawers full of these nice, warm sweaters if she'd moved to Sun City? she thought. They probably had good resale value at the nearby high-end consignment store, true, but it was difficult for her to find warm-weather clothes that she thought looked good on her older body.

Meryl was wearing a new red sweater the day a young woman, holding a detached car seat, asked for a key to a study room she'd reserved. An even younger and smaller woman—almost a girl—with bobbed brown hair who looked familiar stood behind her, arms crossed, one earbud in. The baby was squawking, and Meryl hoped these young women wouldn't assume that the study rooms were soundproof. Sound resistant, yes, but Meryl had had to tell tutors and students to lower their volume. But she handed over the key without saying a word, and continued to browse her hard copy of Library Journal.

She looked up when she remembered where she'd seen the girl: at the lake a month or so ago, at the end of the fall colors. Or rather the marshy pond adjacent to the lake. The girl had been sitting on a wooden bench looking out. She'd been pregnant then, Meryl remembered—a belly that look enormous on such a slight figure—which was why Meryl looked up and through the glass walls of the study room to the baby who must be hers. It was a legal visitation, Meryl realized. Sometimes people came to the library for them. The girl was still not holding the baby, just standing there, looking at the child. The other woman lifted the baby and placed it in the girl's arms. The girl immediately sat, as though the baby was heavy, then touched her nose to the baby's head. Meryl looked away, embarrassed, as the gesture seemed so intimate, and also contrasted the listlessness in the girl both at the pond and a few minutes ago in front of her.

None of Meryl's children had children, and probably wouldn't, since the youngest, Lucy, was single and thirty-five. Meryl was fine with that; she'd never needed grandkids. It sometimes bothered Rick. He'd wanted what he considered a normal life: marriage, house, job, kids, retirement, grandkids. The layoff had robbed him of a traditional retirement, but Meryl had heard him talk on the phone to Lucy about his desire for grandkids. Lucy lived in LA, where many people had kids later in life, so who knows, maybe Rick would receive them. Meryl wondered whether that had been another appeal of Arizona, to be closer to Lucy and potential grandchildren.

Meryl looked into the study room again. The girl was holding the baby closer now, looking down at her, but her shoulders twitched, then hunched whenever the young woman said something. It reminded Meryl of the nervous energy of the squirrels at the lake, their twitching if you came close, their bolting if you came even closer. The girl wanted to bolt with her baby, Meryl could see that. What had this frightened girl done to end up here?

The next morning, Meryl bundled up and carefully walked the snowy and icy path around the lake to the pond. She'd been to the pond more since Rick had left: he hadn't liked to take the detour there. She still missed him just as much, even though she'd thought the acute loss of his presence might have faded just a bit by now, three months in. If he'd died, the grief would have been completely different, but he was still alive and well, just distant from her. But she liked how in her solitude she could take these detours without his resistance. Huge dried-up stalks stretched to the gray horizon on the left side of the pond; the right side seemed mostly frozen over. The turtles she'd seen in the fall, as far as she could tell, weren't there. She sat on the bench where the girl had sat and looked into the winter landscape, a landscape she'd always loved for its barrenness. Sun City, she thought. People in Sun City probably took spring for granted without this preceding frigidness.

The girl continued her visitations at the library through the winter. Once a month, then every other week. She became more comfortable interacting with the baby, though she still seemed reserved, even hesitant outside the study room. The baby went through a louder period in January, and once Meryl had to ask them to quiet her down or leave. The girl immediately tried to hush the baby—probably because if Meryl had kicked them out, she wouldn't see her child again for two weeks. By March, the girl was arriving before the baby, asking for the key from Meryl to let herself in. Meryl and the girl became familiar to each other but didn't chat; the girl simply asked for the key while keeping one earbud in, then Meryl gave it to her.

On some Saturday mornings Meryl walked around the lake with a girl friend Susan, who was about to retire from teaching. Susan said she hadn't felt such elation since she was about to graduate high school. Meryl willed herself to feel like that, too, but she couldn't or didn't want to. She was planning her sideyard garden, but other than that, and looking forward to the lake opening for summer boat rentals, she didn't dream much into the future. Meryl kept an eye out at the lake for the girl, and she did see her once, in February, on a jog wearing a maroon stocking cap with both earbuds in. She nimbly jumped around the snow patches on the path. Youth was amazing, Meryl thought. To have a baby and six months later be able to do that. Her own right ankle still smarted sometimes from where she'd twisted it as she helped Rick move boxes to his truck.

She and Rick talked on the phone about once a week and texted each other photos. For Christmas, Lucy visited him; Jared, their oldest, and his spouse visited her; while Noah, the middle child, went to his in-laws. Jared thought she'd be joining Rick after she turned sixty-seven, and when she told him no, this separation was probably permanent, he seemed confused. "I don't want to live in Arizona," she said, and Jared, who lived in Missoula, said he didn't blame her. But when he asked for the details, and she said they hadn't started divorce proceedings, he said, "Oh so it's still up in the air?" and to let him know what and when they decided. "You sound like a couple of teenagers."

Meryl wondered how old the girl at the library was. As young as sixteen and old as twenty-two, she guessed. Either way, a young mother, especially these days. She hoped the girl hadn't done anything to harm her daughter—she wanted to think her better than that—but you never could tell. In the eighties and nineties, as Meryl was raising her own kids, she'd come across stories of mothers harming or killing their children, and experienced an unusual rage. But if the girl was seriously unstable, the state probably wouldn't let her see her daughter.

As for her and Rick, as Jared had said, they needed to divide assets. It had been six months, and although they hadn't seen each other, they sometimes said "miss you" or "wish you were here." A slow separation was inevitable after over forty years together. But she supposed they should finalize a divorce soon.

In April the girl didn't show for maybe three weeks, then she came on a Wednesday afternoon instead of a Saturday afternoon, her headphones resting around her neck, and asked for the key. "I haven't seen you lately," Meryl said.

"I got a new job," the girl said. "I work weekends now."

"That's too bad."

"I like the new job better." She flashed Meryl something like a smile, pulled the key off the counter, and turned toward the study room.

On her days off, Meryl busied herself in her greenhouse, one of her favorite spaces. The first few years in the house, she'd placed seedlings on the porch roof, the top of a clear plastic umbrella over them as a makeshift greenhouse. When Lucy was in middle school, Meryl had bought a twelve-by-eight-foot walk-in glass greenhouse, which now perpetually smelled like soil. She loved stepping into the warmth of it in early spring. It wasn't until many seedlings had sprouted that she realized she'd planned enough produce for two people, not one. She thought she'd give the extra to coworkers or Susan or another friend or donate them to a food bank. She wasn't going to toss the seedlings now. She and Rick neglected to call each other for a couple weeks and she missed him, but thought that healthy; maybe they were becoming used to their separation.

In June, the lake's municipal boat shed opened, and Meryl enthusiastically rented canoes, as she did every summer, often while Rick went golfing. She could row around the edge of the lake in less than a half hour. When Susan, newly retired, accompanied her, Susan preferred they sit, paddles up, and watch the rabbits, ducks, geese, heron, fish, or swaying branches. "This summer is for rest," Susan told her. "And in the fall, I plan retirement."

Meryl tried to see beyond that summer into her own fall retire-ment, but saw only her side-yard garden: the peas and beans, now ready for harvest, the ripening cucumbers on the vines. She and Rick had planned to visit their kids for extended periods, and had discussed joining a local hiking club, a hobby that had appealed to them but they'd never done. She texted Rick about the hiking club, and he said that he'd seen one down there, and maybe if she moved down, they could sign up? She reminded him that she'd always dreamed of hiking in the mountains, not the desert.

In August, Meryl was standing in her canoe within the cattails on the north side of the lake, craning to see what she thought was a nest, when another canoe, paddled by three tween boys, smacked into her. Meryl stumbled and tripped over one bar in the canoe and crashed into the other. "Oh my god," one boy said. She felt pain in her face, her chest, and her ankles, which she knew she'd reinjured. "Is she knocked out?" another boy said. She mouthed a no, then maneuvered into the middle of the canoe, where she sat on the bottom in a puddle of water. "You OK?" the third boy asked. She shook her head and asked them to pull her canoe to shore. At the dock, two teen boys who worked in the boat shed pulled her out. It was all she could do not to cry out at the pain. Sitting on the dock, without thinking, she called Rick, but hung up when he answered. What could he do for her from there? She called Susan, then another friend, but couldn't reach either. Teens, families, and couples obliviously walked by her to board a canoe or paddleboat. Every time the dock bowed from their movement or weight, her whole hurt body quivered. And then the girl from the library was there, looking down at her.

"Are you OK? Do you need a ride?" she asked. Meryl nodded. Another, taller girl stepped out from behind her. They helped her

hobble to an old green Honda. At the urgent care only a few minutes' drive away, they brought out a wheelchair and pushed her
in, but by the time she'd stood, braced herself against the check-
in counter, and looked over to say thank you, the girls were gone.

Her right ankle was sprained in three places, her left in one.
She had bruising on her torso and face. She took a week off from
work and slept in the spare room downstairs. Over the phone,
Rick said it sounded as though two weeks off was necessary, and
Meryl said "maybe," as she did when she planned not to take his
advice. "You're going back after one, aren't you?" he said, and
asked if she wanted him to fly up to help her. "Lucy is already on
her way," Meryl said, "but thank you." Lucy tried to convince her
to stop working now, to retire early, but Meryl said she'd retire as
planned in October. "I guess I know where I got my stubborn-
ness," Lucy said, then went outside for more tomatoes. It was
a record season for them. When Meryl returned to the library,
wearing a shoe with a flat, immobile sole on her left foot, a full
boot on the right, the bruising hadn't completely faded from
her face, but the girl, when she dropped by the reference desk on
Wednesday to get the key, didn't acknowledge the incident. Out
of context, maybe? Meryl thought. She knew how self-absorbed
young people could be, but she thought this girl was more self-
aware? But no. For the first time, Meryl thought she might join
Rick in Arizona. There was nothing new for her here.

In September, a month before her retirement, the City of Laforge
started a three- or four-month process of draining the lake to
replace a faulty valve. No one seemed to know how it would affect
the critters. She sent both Rick and Susan—who was wandering
cross-country in her newfound freedom—photos of the lowering

water. Susan simply sent her back a photo of Crater Lake, a response Meryl thought cheeky, but Rick reminded her the city had drained the lake twenty years ago, when Lucy was in high school.

I forgot that, she texted back. Then, How would you like some company in Sun City this winter?

Over the phone, Meryl told Rick she'd come just till March, then she wanted to return to experience some of the Front Range's late winter—that her new plan was to spend a half year there and a half year here. She said she'd like him to join her for some or most of the six months in Colorado too, and he said that although he was liking Sun City and he preferred one primary residence, he'd think on it; that he'd also greatly missed her and their life together.

"I won't be here the next time you visit," Meryl said on her last Wednesday at the library as she set the key across the counter. The girl was coming every week now. It was the third semiconversation Meryl had had with her. "My husband and I are moving to Arizona for our retirement." The lie was slight but there.

"It's warmer there," the girl said.

"I wish you the best," Meryl said. For some reason, she felt tears rising. It was strange. She pursed her lips, controlled her tear ducts and face.

The girl looked surprised at the attention Meryl was showing her. "Sometimes that's all you can do. Wish someone the best."

Meryl looked down at her catalogue, her mouth twitching, willing the conversation she'd unwisely initiated to be over.

The girl put a small, smooth hand on top of Meryl's vein-ridden one. "I wish you the best too," she said.

Meryl looked up, but the girl was walking away, her eyes on the glass-walled room where she'd soon meet her daughter.

Meryl was on a break when the girl left the library, and two weeks later, she was en route to Sun City. She never saw the girl again, but sometimes thought of her.

# STRANGERS

■-■-■

On one of the last days of August, Nathan headed into the mountains after work. He coasted through town, then out of it, orange boulders on his right, a creek on his left, and as he drove higher, he saw wildflowers. After he'd passed the town of Nederland, he turned down a gravel road, plunged through an aspen grove, then dipped into a valley, scrubby bushes on either side. The decent gravel became potholed gravel after a mile. The potholed gravel became, after another mile or two, just dirt and potholes. His Jeep could handle the rough roads, but the bouncing revived an upper back injury. At the bottom of the ravine, he pulled over. As he got out, he noticed a miner's shack and a nineties silver Corolla beyond a grove of trees.

Sometimes physical movement made his back feel better, so he walked down the road and back. That didn't help, so he popped a couple ibuprofens and lay on the ground between his Jeep and a blooming cactus. He breathed deeply, closing his eyes as the pain lessened.

When he opened them, a small woman with long, scraggly

black-gray hair stood above him. She wore jeans and a red sweat-shirt with a very faded, cracked white logo on it, and squinted, arms against her chest.

"I'm OK," he said. "Just stretching the back."

"How'd you get down here?" she asked.

It felt as though she was accusing him, he thought. Well, maybe she was a squatter or back-to-the-lander. He could be invading her space.

He sat up and nodded toward the Jeep. His wife had died two years ago, and since then, he'd spent dozens of late afternoons driving around simply because he didn't want to go home.

"How long have you lived out here?" he asked.

"Two years."

"Must be difficult to live without neighbors," he said, standing.

She stepped back, as though threatened by his five-foot-two figure. He wasn't used to that kind of response from anyone, women included.

"It's OK once you get used to it," she said.

"Mind if I take a look at your homestead?"

"I guess not."

She ushered him slightly in front of her as they walked around the shack and over to a garden. Zucchini vines covered an entire plot, which was outlined by a fence of stacked and weaved branches. To the side of the garden was an old picnic table, on which lay a pile of zucchinis, a grater, and large Ziploc bags.

"My garden, my house," she said, pointing. Then, "Excuse me, I've got to finish this." She plopped at the table and started grating.

He looked at the high rock faces on either side of the valley, then up the steep, potholed road from which he'd come. He felt as though he'd entered another world. But wasn't that the point of his aimless driving: to experience another reality, if only for a few hours?

He stepped to the table. "Need a hand with anything around here? I'm pretty handy."

She squinted at him again. "I'm OK," she said. "Just getting ready for a freak snowstorm."

Down in the foothills, where he lived, winter was the last thing on people's minds. But up here there could be snow. He sat across from her. The shape of the grated zucchini reminded him of the maggots in the dumpster behind the factory where he worked. He'd seen them earlier, slithering through waste. He'd gagged, then had gone inside and told the other guys that they'd multiplied.

"By the way," he said. "I'm Nathan."

"Julie," she said, not looking up.

He asked what brought her out here. He thought of his own neighbors, how they all had a good rapport with one another. He imagined telling Kevin at the corner house tonight about the maggots, how his boss, Gus, had overhead the complaints and yelled that goddammit, he couldn't control the hot weather. Kevin would say that ever since the recession Gus had been a son of a bitch, and Nathan would feel a little better.

"I'm on a wait-list for low-income housing in Boulder," Julie finally said. "I might as well wait out here."

Nathan felt lucky he and Anne had bought decades ago, when housing was cheaper. He wondered, if they'd divorced, as he'd suggested twice in the months before her fatal car accident, whether he'd be the one renting now.

"Free rent out here," he said.

She grabbed a handful of grated zucchini and stuffed it into a bag. "But you've got to have a lot of know-how."

"I can imagine."

"I drive into Nederland once a week, if I'm not snowed in, to check the internet at the library, to see if my status has changed. Still fifty people ahead of me."

"After two years?"

"It was 150."

"Let me help you with that," Nathan said.

"All done." Julie stepped over the bench and hoisted the four plastic bags into her arms. "Be right back."

He followed her halfway to her door, but she kept glancing back at him. She didn't want him in there and she didn't like to be followed, he thought, so he dropped into the dirt and did some back stretches.

A few minutes later he heard her heading toward him.

"Don't step on me," he said.

For the first time since he arrived, she smiled. "What's with your back?"

"It's an old injury," he said. "From when I worked construction." Anne had nursed him after the construction accident, then encouraged him to use the settlement money to learn a trade. He ended up going to school to be a barber. They were getting on well then, and he wanted to please her.

She nodded. "Do you want some food?"

It had to be dinnertime. He hadn't noticed that. "If it won't put you out."

"Come on in."

Again, she ushered him slightly in front of her. Her shack had a single bed on the left, a kitchenette on the right, a table under a window, and a woodstove in the middle. "Just the essentials," she said as she headed toward the kitchenette. She was taking deep breaths but didn't look over her shoulder.

"I was gonna have oatmeal for supper, but for a guest, I'll make fish," she said. "And oatmeal on the side."

"No need to go to all that."

"I caught the fish," she said.

While she worked, his hands felt restless. He stepped to the woodstove and opened it. He arranged kindling in a tepee with newspaper underneath, and when Julie didn't comment on it, he lit the stack.

She arranged food on the table, and brought over the stool from the woodstove for herself. Oatmeal, fish, sautéed zucchini. They ate as the inside and outside light dimmed. She told him this was the time of day when she shot rabbits, though of course they didn't come near the shack anymore. She told him she was worried that this winter, her third, would do her in. "I wasn't cut out to live out here."

"Alone?" Nathan asked.

"Just in general. I'm a city person. It felt like learning a new language, and even now, I'm dreading winter."

It dawned on him he could rent her a room for really cheap in his bungalow. He had two bedrooms full of junk. But that would be strange. He didn't even know her.

After they ate, he took the dishes to the counter. She said to leave them, that she'd wash them later. He asked her again if there was anything she needed him to do before he left. "I could even cut your hair."

She smiled at him for the second time.

"I'm a barber," he said. "Trained as one anyway." He'd never set up shop. It was laziness, pure and simple. Anne had said that, and she was right.

Julie stood up and pulled her long hair over her shoulder to look at it. "Oh, I'm OK," she said. "It's more acceptable for older women to have long hair these days. It might need trimmed sometime . . ."

She trailed off as he stepped to her. "It would look nice cut to here," he said, touching her collarbone. And then for some reason he kissed her. She didn't resist, but they both stepped back after. Then she approached him, and after another step back, he stopped. They kissed near the stove, then she led him to the narrow bed. The last time he'd been with a woman on such a small bed was a decade ago, when he, Anne, and their two teenage sons had rented a guard station cabin at the last minute. He and Julie fit fine; Nathan wasn't much heavier now, and Julie was smaller than Anne had ever been. His back hurt at first, but once aroused, he didn't notice it. After, his whole body felt relaxed.

Julie smiled more at the ceiling than at him. "Thank you. I needed that."

Nathan thought he should get dressed and be going, but he pulled the blanket to his chin instead. "You know," he said, "I didn't even like my wife that much." He imagined his neighbor Kevin's face if he'd said that to him, full of surprise and judgment. But Julie had lifted herself up to an elbow. "She was a principal," he said. "So accomplished. I'd always resented her. And it had started to outweigh the love until I couldn't feel the love anymore. Not until after she died."

"I know what you mean," Julie said. "My ex and I . . . I love him but can't be near him. It was not a good relationship."

Nathan wondered about her hesitancy with his movements.

Had her ex abused her? Julie rolled onto her back again. He kissed her on the neck, then all over, more tenderly this time.

After they finished, she hopped up naked and restocked the fire. "In winter," she said, "I wake up from cold and restock it every couple hours."

Again, Nathan thought of asking her to rent one of his rooms, but especially now, that would be weird. "I have an extra room," he said. "If you want to stay in it."

She looked over. "Would I pay in sex?"

"No," he said, embarrassed. "I was thinking about it before all that . . . I'd want you to rent it, but you don't need to pay much."

"I'm not ready to live with a man again," she said. The answer was so immediate and firm he knew she wouldn't change it.

He got up and put on his clothes. "I'll give you the address in case it gets bad out here," he said.

Julie put another piece of firewood in the stove as he wrote it out on a scrap of paper from his wallet. It seemed old-fashioned, he thought, but they had no signal out here, no way to exchange texts.

After he handed it over, her shoulders relaxed. "St. Anth," she said. "My ex lives in Boulder."

"Some Boulder people aren't the best," he said. He wanted to say more, but she'd turned away, her shoulders hunched again, so he left it at that.

Outside, the temperature had dropped, and Nathan shivered in his white T-shirt as he hurried to the car. His Jeep sounded loud as he drove out of the valley. He took two turns he knew, then one he thought he knew, then stopped the car, perplexed. He didn't remember this area, but of course the landscape would look different driving out than driving in. He tried to discern where he was by turning his Jeep around, but that didn't help. He had an emergency kit with him that included a blanket. He could always sleep in his car and drive out in the morning, he thought, even though that would be bad for his back.

He glimpsed Julie watching him from below, then she turned and went inside. He didn't want to ask her for directions, especially at dusk. Even after their intimacy, she might be more skittish at this time of day, if her ex had been the violent type. He turned his car around again and started up the road. As long as he continued to go up, he was headed out of the valley, he figured. He turned on his brights to help him try to avoid the potholes. Gravel began to crunch beneath his tires.

# MIDDLE AGE

———

At Valerie's last inspection of the day, her final stop of every workday, one of the factory workers, Carlos, invited her to join a few guys after work at a local diner. He said his girlfriend, Monica, was meeting him there. Valerie had chatted with Monica a couple times, and liked her, and needed to kill an hour before she picked up her little sister, Amber, at the Denver Airport, so she agreed.

Monica didn't arrive till Valerie was almost done with her pancakes and eggs, but Valerie still smiled and invited Monica to sit across from her. As a former realtor, Valerie had advised Monica on when to put her house on the market, and after they exchanged greetings, Valerie asked how that was going.

"Pending," Monica said.

"Great. And you found a larger place?"

"Yes. In Edmont." Monica handed over photos of it on her phone that Valerie swiped through while Monica looked over the menu, then ordered at the counter. Carlos informed Valerie that the new place had a finished basement as well as two bedrooms on the main floor. He made it sound as though he was moving with her, but when Valerie had discussed it with Monica last fall, Monica said she wanted more space because her daughter, Reina, who'd graduated from college a couple years ago, might move back in.

When Monica returned, Valerie asked whether Reina had received the cancer research job she'd been applying for.

"Yes." Monica beamed. "It's with patients, not in a lab, but it's a good first step."

They discussed the pros and cons of majoring in biology: Reina had majored in it at CSU, Valerie at UC Boulder, and Valerie's teenage son Eli was interested in studying it.

They paused as Monica dug into an omelet. Carlos had one arm around his girlfriend's chair, but was chatting with some guys at the next table, attentive and full of bravado at once. Valerie thought Monica might be too good for him, but sympathized: it was difficult to find unattached, decent men from your mid-thirties on. After Valerie's divorce, she'd paired with a snowboarder in his twenties off and on for a couple years.

Valerie and Monica's conversation transitioned to *Downton Abbey*, which they'd discussed the last time they'd seen each other. Valerie had given up on it—it had become too much like a soap opera for her in season 4—but Monica had continued to enjoy the characters. All the men had left by the end of this discussion, except for Carlos, who was loudly chatting at the front counter with the owner.

"It was good to see you," Monica told Valerie. "Maybe we could get together again? Without the guys?"

As they exchanged numbers, Valerie felt a possibility that her life these days lacked. In her twenties, she'd started several friendships with people in her real estate office, but now, because of the nature of her work or because she was getting older, making new friends was rare.

At the airport pickup, Amber was wearing a gold sweater, her dark hair in a high bun. She'd had upright posture even before she'd entered the Air Force. She put her suitcase in the trunk, then slid into the passenger's side. "Still heading straight to Laramie, right?" she asked as she clicked her seatbelt.

"Yeah," Valerie said, and pulled off the curb.

Amber had asked to join Valerie on her road trip from Denver to their hometown of Hillsboro, a suburb west of Portland, Oregon, where Valerie planned to sign her car over to their mom. Amber said it would be a celebration of her freedom after thirteen years of active duty. After some thought, Valerie acquiesced; she'd been looking forward to driving alone, to listening to music and spacing out, but she and Amber hadn't left their dad's funeral, almost a year ago, on good terms, and Valerie hoped Amber's request might also mean she wanted to reconcile from that.

"It's strange being out," Amber said as they sped up I-25. "I keep thinking I'm on leave or something."

"Yeah, I can imagine," Valerie said. "It'll become real after a few months, I bet." Not for the first time, Valerie wondered why Amber had resigned from the Air Force, when her little sister used to say she'd retire from there.

At the Laramie hotel, Valerie took a shower. She always felt grimy after work—she inspected all kinds of facilities as a USDA agent—and wished she'd had enough time to drive to her own home west of Denver and clean herself before she picked up her sister.

After Valerie got out, Amber suggested going down to the hotel bar and restaurant together, but Valerie declined.

"Oh are you trying not to go to bars?" Amber asked. "No pressure."

Her little sister had been that sensitive after their dad's funeral, too, eyeing Valerie whenever the family passed around a bottle of wine. Amber hadn't known about Valerie's addiction to pills until after their dad had been diagnosed with late-stage prostate cancer and the sisters were texting more. To Amber, the addiction might feel recent, though to Valerie, after six years of being clean, it usually felt in the past.

"No, I go to bars," Valerie said. "Just kinda tired."

Amber went down without her.

Valerie lay in bed texting Eli, fell asleep, then woke to Amber coming back in. Her sister undressed and slipped into the bed next to hers. Like their childhood room, Valerie thought. Two beds, with lamps in between. The last time they'd slept in the same room was when Valerie had left baby Eli with John, her then husband, and she and Amber had stayed a night at a motel in Palisade after a day of wine tasting to celebrate Amber's graduation from the Air Force Academy. Now, Valerie felt regret that they hadn't kept in touch after that, while she was a busy realtor with a young child and Amber had been deployed.

The next morning at the continental breakfast, Amber zoned out to the news on TV, while Valerie checked several sites for the strength of wind gusts off I-80.

"It's looking like about fifty mile per hour gusts today," she told Amber.

"OK," Amber said.

It probably seemed like nothing in comparison to her experiences overseas, Valerie thought. "I'm just glad we're in a sedan," she said. "We'll rock less than in a high cab."

Amber nodded, then stood. "Would you like a coffee to go?"

"Yes please," Valerie said.

They were on the road by 8:30. Valerie started an eighties playlist and thought she'd allow them to settle into the drive before she initiated a conversation, but within thirty minutes, the wind was shaking the car. If she let go of the wheel for a split second, she thought, the gusts might fling them into the other lane.

"Are you doing anything for your fortieth?" Amber asked.

"I'm just trying to focus on the road."

Amber waved a hand. "I'm trying to distract you from this."

"No plans right now."

"Do you want to do something in a group or alone?"

"I haven't thought about it." Valerie tightened her grip on the wheel.

"Remember, in high school, you were obsessed with Finland after we found out Mom's grandma was from there? You could travel there."

Valerie knew her little sister wasn't trying to remind her that Amber had traveled all over while Valerie had never been out of the continental United States, but she thought of it, nonetheless.

"The fall would be a pretty time to be there," Amber continued.

"I'll think on it," Valerie said. She now had enough money for a trip overseas, though these days, she was obsessed with France, not Finland.

The wind pushed them toward the center lane, and Valerie grimaced as she fought her way back.

"And if I'm around," Amber said, "you can give me a list of friends, and I'll throw a party."

That offer seemed overly generous, Valerie thought. Insincere within their current relationship. Maybe it was just something to say so the weather wouldn't overwhelm them. "What are you plans anyway?" Valerie asked. "Are you settling around here? I mean, in Colorado?"

"I never fell for the Rockies like you did. Maybe Oregon. Or at least the Northwest."

Valerie nodded. So Amber wouldn't be around to throw her a party. Then why had she said that? Overcompensation maybe? Valerie sped up to over eighty, though she'd read online to drive slowly in such high winds. Amber grabbed the door handle, and part of Valerie felt glad for her sister's nervousness.

"I think you should slow down," Amber said.

Valerie did slightly. The strength of the wind lessened, but Valerie, not wanting to talk, turned up the music.

"We should be out of Wyoming in another hour," Amber said. She was following their progress on her phone.

"Good," Valerie said. "I'm done with this state." She forgot about the incessant open spaces in the West when in Denver or Portland or flying, but felt them deeply the few times she'd been on the road between the two.

"Fuck," Valerie said as the wind intensified.

"You want me to drive?" Amber asked.

Valerie shook her head.

"There's a lot of cheap land for sale in Wyoming," Amber said. Trying again, Valerie knew, to distract from the weather.

"But who wants to live here?" Valerie said.

"People used to think that about Forest Grove too. Remember the homestead?" Amber smiled. "We could've been farmers."

"Or millionaires," Valerie said.

Their dad's grandpa had owned a 160-acre plot in Forest Grove, near Hillsboro, then sold it off during the Great Depression. Nike and Intel facilities had moved in near the plot, which pushed real estate prices way up. Valerie's own house in Golden had more than doubled in value since she and John bought it, but she was unable to remain levelheaded when it came to her own real estate career: after the crash, she had a panic, a mind block; she couldn't imagine prices improving. Then she tore her ACL on the slopes, and something in her brain broke or she chose to go off the rails. Probably a little of both.

Look at Amber, Valerie thought. Despite the wind gusts, she was relaxed. As far as Valerie knew, her sister hadn't had one breakdown, despite being in two wars. She realized she was going over eighty again, and slowed down. It was not healthy to compare herself to someone else, she reminded herself. And it had taken her both strength and vulnerability to recover.

As they reached Utah, the wind died down for good, and after they stopped to use the bathroom and get food, Amber took over at the wheel. The difficult driving conditions had taken it out of Valerie; she didn't feel like conversing with her sister. There was always tomorrow, she figured.

At an Idaho Falls hotel, she again opted to stay in the room while Amber went down to the restaurant and bar. She wanted to get room service, she told Amber. It was a luxury for her. She called Eli while she waited for the delivery, then channel-surfed over the meal, stumbled across reruns of *Downton Abbey*, and thought of Monica. Maybe she'd try to finish the show, Valerie thought. She did really like the clothes.

The next morning, both Valerie and Amber overslept, and rushed to be on the road by ten. It was almost nine hours to Hillsboro, and they wanted to spend quality time with their mom before she went to bed. "She's stayed up to chat with us on work nights before," Amber said.

"Yes, but she's getting older," Valerie said.

As they drove through Boise on the freeway, they discussed how they'd heard the city had changed, and people from their high school who'd settled there. Valerie felt more at ease with her sister today, and thought that if to discuss impersonal topics without hostility was as far as their relationship progressed on this trip, maybe that was OK.

They filled up their gas tank west of Boise, in Nampa, and Amber took over driving. They neared the Oregon border. "*Only* four hundred miles to go," Valerie said.

The hills of the Eastern Oregon desert gave way to the plains near Pendleton, a town famous for its blankets and rodeo, then they reached the Columbia River. "We'll need to get gas one more time probably," Amber said.

"I'll keep an eye out."

They were silent then, and Valerie took in the power lines, windmills, and water. The width and beauty of the Columbia surprised her for an hour or two, then she became restless as they neared Portland; the highway with water alongside it felt like it would last forever.

"We're getting pretty low," Amber said.

"There's been nothing."

"I know. I'm just saying."

Valerie glanced at the gas gauge. Soon, she was grabbing the door handle, as Amber had the day before.

"How many miles till The Dalles?" Amber asked.

Valerie keyed it into her phone. "Thirty-one."

"I forgot there aren't any gas stations around here."

Valerie got out her Triple A card. By the time they came to a complete stop at the side of the highway, she had the number up. She dialed as Amber stepped out of the car, then joined her a few minutes later. "Ninety minutes or so till they arrive," she said.

"I'll let Mom know," Amber said.

Valerie sat next to her, and they looked at the orange and pink light against the wide river. Valerie's mind went blank; she had nothing she wanted to discuss with Amber. She remembered calling her sister almost every week when Amber was in the academy, and every time, they'd talk for hours. How was that possible? Valerie thought. What in God's name did they discuss for hours? It seemed as though ever since she'd become clean she could remember in images but not specifics. When the water went dark, she stood and got back in the car, while Amber stayed sitting on the incline facing the river.

They reached the eastern sprawl of Portland at nine. Valerie felt a strong desire to see their mom as they drove the freeway bridge above the lit-up skyscrapers. "Did you miss home?" she asked. "Is that why you decided to resign from the Air Force?"

Amber didn't reply. They sped through Beaverton, a suburb.

"You want to get coffee?" Valerie said. "Los Lobos is still open till ten, I think. My treat. Mom might want one too, if we're gonna stay up."

Again, Amber didn't reply. She had no more of an idea why Amber might resign, Valerie thought, than Amber had of why she herself had become an addict. They'd missed years of each other's lives, and simply answering these kinds of questions now would not make up for that. "You awake?" Valerie said.

"I think I want to hang out with Mom a few minutes alone," Amber said. "Maybe you could drop me off, then get us all coffee? It was nice of you to offer."

"OK," Valerie said.

She didn't speak again as she exited the highway, drove the streets into town, then dropped off Amber in their parents' driveway. On Hillsboro's Main Street, she pulled into a parking spot along the curb but remained sitting in the car.

She could live forty more years, she thought, and the reoccurring images from the first half of her life would remain: Amber lying on the ground under her swing in a schoolyard less than a mile from here trusting her older sister to keep her knees locked as she swooped over so she wouldn't hurt her; the infectious smile of Valerie's first love—a high school guy with a locker next to hers—who lent her Michael Creighton books; the charismatic, sweet young woman on a Greyhound from Portland to Eugene who convinced Valerie to go to college in Boulder; meeting John on the rocks above a creek the summer after she graduated from UC; the sunlight shining onto the cream carpet of the living room the day John found her high while she was supposed to be watching Eli; last year, walking on this sidewalk with Amber, Amber saying she wished Valerie had told her about her addiction sooner. "I'm not as strong as you," Valerie had said, walking ahead. "I couldn't have been where you've been without PTSD. But maybe that's a good thing. Maybe I'm not incapable of feeling." And Amber had come up close from behind and said, "You don't know what you're talking about," then about-faced and walked away, and until the Denver Airport two days ago, that was the last time they'd seen each other. It was as though they'd been five and eight, not thirty-five and thirty-eight, and instead of holding up her legs while swinging, Valerie had dropped them, kicking her sister in the face.

Valerie wanted to empty her brain of these memories. She also knew to do that would be doing away with her core. There were people in your life, she thought—sometimes family, sometimes strangers; sometimes friends, sometimes lovers—that you connected with on such a deep level that it made life worth living. Sometimes you connected with them once, sometimes for a few years, sometimes for your whole life. It was the only thing that had made any sense to her, these connections, though the randomness of them and loss of them didn't.

In a couple of days, she'd fly home, Valerie thought. And it would be relaxing not to be in the confined space of the car with her sister. Maybe, in the future, her and Amber's relationship would revive. But that took two people—though she was probably the reluctant one, not Amber.

On her phone, Valerie scrolled to Monica's number. I've been eyeing that Italian restaurant in St. Anthony, she texted. Would you like to meet up sometime there?

# PAVEL

●━●━●

Every day I sat on the curb in front of my apartment complex smoking, watching cops do their rounds, while pot sat between my feet in a brown paper bag. My favorite time for customer pickup was early morning, when the light felt hopeful, and I was one of the few people out on County Road. This happened only once or twice a week, since most people were asleep then, and most customers thought cops were less likely to spot them later in the day. I went along with whatever customers wanted, within reason, though if asked, I'd tell them the cops probably knew but pretended not to. I didn't sell pills, coke, or heroin, only pot and shrooms.

In December of 2019 I made the mistake of bringing a customer home. In my defense I was in my thirties, and most guys on apps like Grindr felt young; many of my friends had a steady partner or had even settled down. So on one of those early mornings, when I sensed attraction between me and a new customer and invited him back to my studio, it felt nostalgic and real, as though I was in my twenties again and bringing someone home from a grocery store or bar while my mom and stepdad were on the road selling meat-stuffed Russian rolls. This guy, Dave, was white, and a few years older and a few inches shorter than I was, and his body was firm: unlike me, he probably worked out. He bought only pot, which was legal in Colorado, and all the drugs in my apartment were out of sight. Still, it was a bad move. Pure laziness.

The second time I brought him home, I told him I could no longer sell to him. He said he understood, that he'd buy pot at a shop, that this was worth it to pay a little more. We met more mornings outside my apartment complex, and after, he'd ride a bus to work. I enjoyed watching him walk down the snow-shoveled sidewalk, his step bouncy, his grin relaxed, his eyes as impossibly blue as the Southwestern sky. He reminded me of a Wyoming boy, their small-town self-sufficiency, the way I thought of all American guys for years after my mom married an American and she and I moved to Richmond, Wyoming, from Ulan Ude, Russia, when I was eleven. And I wondered if I was attracted to Dave, or only the idea of him, that he reminded me of the first boys I'd loved.

I was surprised when weeks in, I still hadn't told him I used to be an English teacher, that I'd become a drug dealer only after I was fired from teaching high school in Richmond when a student saw a bong in my trunk. Usually, if someone talked to me more than twice I'd tell them the story. I even told my neighbor Pete, who sometimes stopped to smoke with me on his morning walk to work. At my old school, I'd been unloading final project folders from my car, and two of my students stopped and asked whether they could help. One of them saw the bong, and tattled on me, and the next thing I knew my car was searched on the final day of my tenth year of teaching, and I ended up not only fired and my teaching license suspended but in jail for a year. I don't know what broke my mom's heart more, me going to jail or me moving down here.

What was I going to do in Richmond, I'd told my mom, without a teaching license, and when everyone in town knew what I'd done? I didn't tell her that it had already been hard enough to keep that I was gay on the down-low in such a conservative town, including around her. So I'd used my savings to rent a studio in St. Anthony, Colorado, and my weed dealer hooked me up with a supplier down here. I missed some friends, my mom and stepdad, and teaching, but I'd liked exploring Denver's gay scene for a couple years. I'd never lived so close to a major city.

Pete said he had a cousin in Arizona with a similar conviction, and that one of the presidential candidates had proposed legalizing pot nationwide and expunging all past records, and after that, for a few mornings before I met Dave, I'd scroll through these policies on my phone and listen to Bernie Sanders's interviews, and think it too good to be true, that something like this could happen, that America could be a "land of opportunity" for me again. That's what my mom called it after I'd fucked up. Couldn't you follow a few laws, she'd asked, to live in a land of opportunity?

I felt a strange vibe with Dave maybe two months in, when he asked me about my Russian background. Especially since I looked Asian, not Slavic, I was used to people being curious about that, but he seemed interested in unusual facts, such as how long my family had lived in Ulan Ude and the names of my relatives. I didn't tell him much at first, just a few innocuous stories from growing up. In retrospect, his fascination should have been a warning sign, but I was blinded by convenience. I'd stopped driving into Denver as much since I'd become friendly with Pete, and if I kept Dave around, I wouldn't need to go there for hookups.

Around the time I met Dave, I began to tutor Pete's girls twice a week. They were in seventh and tenth grade, and while Pete and I were smoking one morning, Pete had mentioned they'd both tested below grade level in reading comprehension. I said I could tutor them, and he said he wasn't hinting at that, but maybe, if I wasn't too busy, that would be great, then when I saw him hesitating, I added that paying me in dinner would be plenty, if that worked for him and his wife.

They lived in a two-bedroom townhouse that shared a wall with my studio. During dinners, I sat at the corner of their small square kitchen table, but didn't mind. The native dishes his wife, Nino, made were by far the best thing I ate every week—Indian tacos, tamales, green chile. After the meal, we'd all clear the table, then Emilee and Bly would bring over their books and the three of us would sit back down. The public schools in St. Anth had nicer and newer textbooks than those in Richmond, but many of the stories were the same: "To Build a Fire," "The Yellow Wallpaper," and so on. The same ones I'd read in high school, the ones that had inspired me to become an English literature major and teacher.

I think I'd latched onto English class to prove to myself that I could adapt after moving to the United States. Or maybe it was because I was an outsider, as both an immigrant and a gay kid, and I needed to channel my rejected energy somewhere. Either way, I'd fallen in love with reading in English. And while attending college in Fort Collins, I wasn't an outsider anymore because

I found other people who liked literature, and when they smoked pot, I smoked pot, and the rest, as Americans say, is history.

After I asked Emilee and Bly questions on their current stories, which I'd always either already taught or read, sometimes I'd drop on the couch in the adjacent room and watch whatever game was on with Pete, and sometimes drink a beer. I didn't like sports much, except for soccer, and he liked most sports, except for soccer, but he didn't mind us sometimes watching it.

I finally told Dave about my arrest in February, after he'd started in on my Russian background. If he was interested in knowing me, I thought, my past in the States was as influential as my past—or my relatives' past—in Siberia. He immediately got weird. How I could break the law, he asked, what kind of role model was I? I said yes I'd been careless to leave the bong in the car, but I wasn't smoking around or with them. He said I seemed above that, to be a teacher and pot smoker at once, and when he left he said "see you around," as though we'd never meet up again. I was surprised at him, even after all my years in the States. I should have internalized that Americans sometimes have random moral hang-ups; for Russians, loyalty to a friend or lover comes first.

By mid-afternoon, when Pete was walking home from work, I was sitting on the curb singing. It was an unusual sight in America, but it had come back to me, how people would belt out songs walking through markets in Ulan Ude. Russian tunes are often in minor keys, mournful, and thus comforting, though not all Americans would think that. I hesitated as I saw Pete, but when he stopped a few feet away, head bowed, as though waiting, I continued to the end of the phrase, then offered him a cigarette.

Dave didn't show for two weeks, then one morning dropped by again. I didn't ask questions, just took him to my place. I probably seemed a bit mad but didn't care. I'd learned that since I didn't live close to anyone who had known me for years, no one was around to call me out for being self-destructive. That day, after sex, he wanted to hear about my relatives, so I told him that my great-grandparents, who were ethnically Buryat, had come to Siberia from Mongolia. I still had a distant cousin in Mongolia that I kept in intermittent contact with. I rolled out of bed and pulled out from a cardboard shipping box a Mongolian football jersey my cousin had just sent me for my thirty-fifth. It was a joke; most of my relatives, including me, were Russian football fans.

I didn't return to bed once I got out, and Dave had asked me while looking at the ceiling. Maybe this is how we'd part ways, I thought, asking more and more intimate questions without intimacy, growing further apart as we learned more about each other. Or maybe only as he learned more about me; I hadn't asked about him. After my monologue, he shrugged into his clothes quickly, and didn't touch me or even make eye contact as we said goodbye. I watched him walk away as I sat on the curb waiting for the next customer, a paper bag between my feet, and thought I wouldn't be surprised if I never saw him again.

In mid-March the pandemic quarantine began. People still bought drugs, more than usual even. It was difficult for me to keep up with demand. In order to practice social distancing, I'd pick up customers' payment off the pavement with gloves, then throw it in a shoebox for twenty-four hours before touching it again. I was still going to Pete's—we figured we'd try to keep whatever virus we might have between our two apartments—but not surprisingly, because of our recent exchanges or the quarantine, I hadn't seen Dave in weeks. In the mornings that I lay in bed alone, I wondered if this pandemic were ever over, and if my record were really expunged, whether I'd return to Wyoming to teach. I thought I probably would—I missed the sparseness of the landscape and some friends and especially during the quarantine missed and worried about my mom—but I'd try for a different school in a different town.

My mom and stepdad didn't know I dealt; they thought I'd been tutoring ever since I moved down to St. Anth. Over the phone, I told my mom that during the quarantine I was tutoring Pete's girls, but had suspended other assignments. She said she was worried that I didn't have enough money coming in, and I said I had money saved, and would be fine. I changed the topic of conversation from myself whenever I could, instructing her on how to properly wear a mask, on how to call the store for grocery pickup. She seemed to be doing fine: my mom laughed that Russia, like China, was underreporting cases and deaths. To stay sane, many post-Soviets have developed a dark sense of humor toward the government.

One evening in early April, as I was helping Emilee and Bly do their assignments, and remembering once again how much I loved literature and sharing my knowledge with others, I heard a harsh knock, I thought on my apartment door. I wondered who it was, especially since we were all supposed to be staying distant from one another, and ignored them, until I heard my door banged in, and voices inside my apartment. I jumped up, and the girls, too, seemed worried, Bly, the younger, looking at me as though asking how to react. "I'll be right back," I told them, feigning confidence.

Whoever was inside my place was in the loft bedroom upstairs.

I sat on the couch since I didn't want to rush up and round the corner to a knife or gun. After a minute, two police officers came down holding my baggies of pot. I was lucky that because of the rush for the first time I had only pot, and only a small amount, on hand. I recognized one of them, a slight Hispanic guy who patrolled the neighborhood. I was pretty sure he knew I dealt. The other was a stocky white guy I'd never seen. I stood as they approached me, my palms open and out because I knew not to be an idiot around pigs.

"Looks like you have a bit more than six ounces," the Hispanic guy said.

I didn't respond or even nod, just stared at him. He knew what he'd found, but I wasn't going to give him more information.

"All right, let's go," the white guy said, motioning toward the door.

"I'm tutoring a couple girls next door," I said. "Can I tell them I'm leaving?"

The white guy laughed, maybe at the incongruity. A drug dealer who was also a tutor. "I guess," he said.

Both Emilee and Bly looked up from the table with expectation. Pete and Nino were also in the kitchen. "The cops found over the legal limit of pot in my apartment," I said. "I have to go to the station with them." The girls weren't toddlers, and could handle this information.

Nino grimaced. Pete just nodded. "Here," he said, "let me give you my number."

I was surprised we hadn't already exchanged them.

The St. Anthony station was small and clean and unintimidating. The only moment that gave me pause was when the white guy, examining my license on a computer screen, said he was surprised I was a citizen. "Why?" I asked. I'd become a citizen when I was seventeen, although I reflected as the cop cleaned my license with a Clorox wipe, then held it out without responding, that wasn't something I'd told Dave. He was probably the one who'd turned me in. Maybe he'd lied, told the police that because of relatives I'd been traveling and had brought back the virus.

The police fined me seven hundred dollars, then let me go, with another blot on my record. And in a state where pot was legal. I was pissed. At my studio, I texted Pete that I was home and OK, but that I should stay away from them for a couple weeks since I'd broken quarantine. I then called my mom. She answered with the Russian alloh; she always assumed the person calling didn't want to speak English. Mostly she talked; I didn't mention my charges. That time of the year, preparing for the main selling season, always excited her. I told her she needed to be careful with COVID spreading. She said she and my stepdad decided not to drive around and set up in different towns, but to offer her meat-stuffed rolls in Richmond as delivery.

I decided to suspend my drug dealing, and cut ties with my supplier and customers. I applied to a Boulder County tutoring agency that for the pandemic had gone online. I had former colleagues in Richmond who'd vouch for my teaching, though the administration wouldn't. When the agency wouldn't hire me after I failed a background check, I advertised on Craigslist and received immediate responses. So many local parents who had kids home from school wanted to do virtual learning on Skype, Google Hangouts, or Zoom. I received enough tutoring to sustain me, but talking to people through a screen all day sometimes felt disembodying, and I was glad when I could return to Pete's.

Since there were no sports on TV, sometimes the whole family and I would play penny poker at the cramped table, or Pete and I would watch eighties or nineties wrestling reruns in the living room. Unlike most Richmond boys, I'd never gotten into wrestling, but Pete didn't seem to care that I didn't know much, so I didn't feel as embarrassed as I had with them.

After I got into a regular online tutoring schedule, and my return to Wyoming had become less likely after Sanders suspended his campaign, my down-time daydreams returned to Dave, anger at him for most likely turning me in, yes, but also some pining. Sometimes in the early mornings I'd go on walks, to a pond about a half mile away, to an open space near a creek over a mile or more. I'd watch the morning light on the ice of the pond, on the water in the creek, not frozen over. Although in Ulan Ude my mom and I had walked everywhere, even across frozen rivers, in the States, I'd never been one to walk for the sake of walking—but now it helped me deal with the early mornings, when I'd enjoyed shooting the shit with Pete and sleeping with Dave. I saw more people in my neighborhood than I ever had before those walks, and we'd wave or nod, and skirt six feet around each other. Once, while out one morning in May, I saw the Hispanic cop patrolling, and nodded to show no hard feelings, and he pulled his cruiser to the curb, rolled down the window, and said they'd had to investigate a tip. "Don't worry about it, man," I said. And my anger at Dave overrode any pining until I didn't register a neighbor had waved until after she'd passed, since I was so inside my head, consumed with hating him.

When some people in Colorado headed back to their offices, I ditched my morning walks, and instead rode the bus down County Road, trying to ride on the same one as Dave. On maybe my fourth or fifth try, on a morning I'd unfortunately forgotten to wear a mask, I saw him sitting in front of me, one row back from the handicapped area, facing ahead, mask on, then I followed him out of the bus and onto the walking-only street in downtown Boulder. Although I'd watched Dave's body every morning that he'd walked toward and away from me, I'd never noticed how fast he walked, or maybe he was simply late for work that day. I had no idea what to say when I reached him. I wanted to confront him, to see his face when he knew I knew he'd turned me in. But when he abruptly veered left, toward a three-story brick building, and I, breathing hard, called his name, and he turned, I didn't know whether I could crack him open.

"Paul," he said, his voice muffled. I'd adopted the name Paul at the beginning of high school, after middle-school boys had relentlessly made fun of Pavel, my Russian name.

"I was on your bus this morning," I said, my breath steadying. "You were in front of me."

He nodded. People wearing masks walked by us in an ebb and flow on the wide brick street. "This is where I work." He gestured his dress-shirted arm to the building.

I felt aware of my face that felt empty without a mask, of my old jeans and T-shirt, and of my body among all these white people passing. This was not the time to yell at him. I'd draw attention to myself, and no doubt someone would chide my mask-lessness. I took two steps back. "Are you going to drop by again?" I asked.

He looked away. "There was the quarantine," he said. "Now work's been wanting me to come in earlier and earlier."

Maybe a lie, maybe not. "What about tomorrow morning?" I asked. "A weekend."

He looked back at me, then shrugged. "Maybe. Maybe I'll come."

I felt stung by his nonchalance, and wanted so badly to confront him, but now I was drawing stares from passersby, whether because of my ethnicity or my lack of mask, I didn't know. I gave him a nod, tried not to act invested. "OK," I said. "See you around."

I was restless the next morning. A quirk of growing older was that I couldn't sleep in. I made coffee, then wondered whether I should make food later for Dave and me. I tried to imagine us eating together but couldn't. I doubted he'd even come.

I was sitting on top of a picnic table in an open area behind the apartment complex, smoking, when Pete came out. I offered him a cigarette and he stood puffing, looking at aspens that led down to a stream, their silver leaves fluttering. I hadn't been over to his place lately; his daughters were on a summer break from remote school so I wasn't tutoring.

"How's work?" I asked. He worked at a factory that had been closed for a month during quarantine.

"It's OK." He shook his head noncommittally. "The factory will probably eventually shut down for good. I'm not sure it will survive the pandemic."

"Wasn't there a federal bailout?"

"My boss is too lazy to apply or didn't qualify or the feds ran out of money or something. You apply?"

"What, as a sole proprietor drug dealer?"

We laughed.

"If it does, we might move back to Arizona," Pete said. "But Nino still has her job, the schools are good here."

"I'd be sad to see you go, man."

"You sticking around?"

"Probably. For now." If I did leave, I didn't know what I'd miss besides Pete and his family, the morning light against pavement or ice or water, the views in certain areas of St. Anthony of the mountains. I hadn't even thought of going to Denver since the bars reopened. "Why'd you move here anyway?"

"My cousin lives here and likes it. Said there were better schools. Some nice people."

He offered me a cigarette, and we smoked another together. I wanted to ask him to hang out at a St. Anth bar now that we could go to them, but pushed aside the impulse. He'd been accepting of me in his apartment, but he and probably his coworkers were much more conservative than my English major friends, and I didn't know whether he'd be comfortable running into one of them if we were out one on one. I didn't want to bring him any grief. It was 9:50 when I went back in.

Someone knocked lightly on my door at 10:15. Dave had never knocked before since I'd always been outside to greet him. I hated the hesitancy in the knock; it reminded me of how he'd probably gone behind my back. I tried to hide my displeasure as I ushered him upstairs with my arm while I greeted him.

Usually our sex was quick and casual, then we lay in bed for a few minutes, talking. That day, I drew out the foreplay, making an almost grotesque display of kissing him. His body recoiled, maybe because I was acting differently, probably because it was more like a scene in a play than passion. At one point he begged me not to press his body so hard against the wall, but I didn't listen.

After, we lay in bed, me on my back, him on his side looking at a wall. "You know, don't you?" he asked.

I said I did. "Why the fuck, man?"

"I got the virus from you. Not a bad case, but still."

I started.

"I can't believe you accepted that package."

I realized he was talking about my jersey. I thought of how most likely the virus wasn't on that package, of all of the other places he could have caught it. "The virus was barely talked about in America then."

"You should have known about it. Being Asian." He rolled out of bed and pulled on his jeans.

I thought of how well Mongolia had done containing the virus, of how I probably should have guessed he was racist before that day, but I hadn't cared enough about him to ask personal questions. I admired his abs one last time before he buttoned his shirt over them.

"Why'd you come over today?" I asked.

"To see if you knew." He gave me that casual Wyoming-boy grin.

I wished I'd been even rougher with him. "Get out of here," I said.

I locked the door after he left, then suddenly felt lightheaded since I hadn't yet eaten.

My phone was on the kitchen counter. Hey, Pete had texted. You wanna come over for dinner?

I'd suggest we sit outside, at the picnic table, I thought. OK, I wrote. Thanks. You want me to bring anything?

I cracked three eggs into a bowl and beat them with milk. My phone lit up.

Just yourself is fine, he'd written.

I can do that, I wrote back.

I forced myself to hum a Russian song as I poured the eggs into a hot, buttered pan. By the time I sat down on my couch to eat them scrambled, I was belting it out. I didn't mind if Pete or his family heard my singing.

# BRATWURST HAVEN

———

**M**eg looked through the thin morning fog at St. Anthony Sausage, trying to imagine what the shop would look like if her father cared about it. No leaves scattered across the concrete walkway. A sign without rust. He would have replaced the three window panes on the second story where cold air seeped into the office.

She stubbed out her cigarette and turned off the truck. She pushed open the heavy door of the shop and walked through the first floor. On her left, workers stood on either side of a metal table, cutting meat off bone. Her father, Gus, paced beside them. He was pacing already, she thought. It was going to be one of his bad days.

Upstairs, in the area that served as both break room and office, she put her sack lunch in the fridge and poured coffee into a gray, ceramic mug. She'd just laid out the punch cards when she smelled something. She turned to Matt, one of the workers. Some of them wore the same clothes all workweek.

"Pay day!" he said. He poured coffee into a Styrofoam cup. He stepped toward her. "You gonna pay us overtime?"

It had become his mantra that fall, ever since two of his buddies quit. He used to complain to them. Now, he complained to her.

She studied his punch card. "I don't think you worked much overtime the past couple weeks, did you?"

"Somewhere between one and five hours."

"It's not up to me."

"You could talk to your dad."

She tilted her head. He was stocky, flabby, and flushed. His baseball cap, underneath his bump cap, was curled. "Has he ever been persuaded to do anything?" she asked.

Matt set his cup on a windowsill. "It was worth a shot."

She ignored the cup and turned to the punch cards. She added up hours in her head and entered them into a notebook and onto computer-generated paystubs on her desktop. The coffee warmed and woke her. Every now and then Gus raising his voice jolted her out of focus. Some workers needed such stern encouragement. And people like Matt or another slacker, Carlos, didn't deserve overtime. But she felt badly for others, like Nathan or Enrique, people who did.

At the end of their day, employees came up to grab their checks. After the office emptied, her father slowly climbed the stairs. "I need to hire someone who knows how to clean up," he said.

"What about Enrique?" she asked.

"Oh he's great but we need one or two more like him."

He complained about Matt's smoke breaks, Honey's laziness. As he paced, his face reddened from the neck up. Finally, he quieted, and turned from her to head home. He didn't know how to run a business, she thought. He had never known.

She arrived home at five o'clock. A chilly breeze rushed at her as she walked from the carport to the single-wide, and she hoped the first snow might fall that night.

In the kitchen, she spiced chicken legs and made a salad. Out the window she could see the ranch house that her fiancé, Caleb, had grown up in and the jagged mountains of the Front Range. They planned to build on this property after they married next summer. Caleb and his dad, who ran a construction business, would oversee it.

When Caleb entered, she greeted him with a kiss. They ate quietly and afterward she sat on his lap while they watched the light fade and discussed their days.

"Why don't you notify the labor board?" he suggested after she said Matt had asked again for overtime. "You're the only one he wouldn't suspect."

She went in to kiss his neck.

"Or you could just pay them. Does your dad check the books?"

She nuzzled into him. "Yeah. If he didn't, I might do that. Legally, we should be."

"Well, if you want to get started on legality . . ."

She put a finger over his lips and he curled a tongue around it. Three of the chain restaurants paid the factory in cash and under the table, she knew that.

"I'll straighten that out if I ever own it."

"Do you want to?" he asked seriously.

"Probably."

"We could have our kids work there. Child labor."

"Just what I had in mind." She knocked off his hat and kissed him.

They made out in front of the window, an orange light beyond them, before they moved to the shadowy bedroom. After they made love, she stood outside in the darkness smoking, thinking over Caleb's suggestion. It had never occurred to her to notify the labor board herself. That she could stop this so effectively and indirectly.

The following Monday, while her dad and the other workers were downstairs, she created a Gmail account and sent the labor board an anonymous email. She included that employees were afraid that they'd be fired if they reported it. At lunch, while her father ate his sandwich, she studied him, his remaining wisps of dirty-blond hair, his surly glances toward Honey, who, they all suspected, brought liquor in her water bottle. He would not suspect her, she thought. Caleb was right.

In the afternoon, because they didn't have many orders to prepare for the next day, Halloween, her dad asked her to take Matt and Pete to one of the storage units they owned behind the shop to clean it out. She unlocked the roller door, and helped the men load scrap wood, broken chairs, and boxes of old paperwork into her pickup.

One of the boxes contained cards and letters from her mother, who had died from breast cancer when Meg was twelve. "Just leave those," she said. "I'll ask about them."

"Sucks we have to organize his personal shit," Matt said.

"He's paying you, isn't he?" she said sharply.

She'd made a point never to commiserate with the workers, even though she sometimes agreed with them. But this aggressive, defensive tone was new, a result of her guilt for reporting on her dad. The men quieted and continued to sort, occasionally asking what should go where.

As they worked, Meg found herself thinking that newer, richer St. Anth residents wouldn't hesitate to rent out units at twice the amount they currently charged. If they cleared out this unit and consolidated the shop stuff, they could rent out four units at a higher price.

After an hour, the tamale lady dropped by. They all gathered around her basket and colorful clothing and pulled out their wallets and looked over her wares.

Meg bought a dozen chicken and a dozen pork. The men bought a half dozen of each. Pete talked to the lady in Spanish, which surprised Meg, who thought he was a Navajo a couple generations removed from the reservation. He never spoke Spanish in the shop.

After the lady left, Meg dismissed the men and hurried home to make a fire with the papers and scrap wood. She built it so high that Caleb said he could see it a mile out. They ate warmed tamales in front of it, then she danced around it like a child while Caleb laughed.

The next evening, she took more tamales to her dad's house. At supper, and in between groups of trick-or-treaters, they discussed the changing downtown. She said she liked Lunar, a newer brewpub; he raged against the closing of Goodie's, a decrepit corner store. He disliked any kind of change, she thought, but she was thankful that they both took an interest in St. Anthony. Besides that, running the business, and some memories of her mother, they had very little in common.

She brought up her idea for the storage units when they were standing on the porch at 9:30, checking for lingerers before they turned out the porch light. Across the way, a cat was cut into a sagging pumpkin. The wind, she swore, smelled like snow. Her chest ached for winter, when small outings into the cold made her feel courageous, and inside became a cozy contrast.

"But then we'd have to raise the prices on all the units," he said.

"Do we?"

"Within a month or two."

She knew he owned the shop out of ease, not love. He'd inherited it, and most of his laziness, incompetence, and impatience came from his dislike of running it.

"I could be in charge of that," she said. "Gradually increase the prices."

"I don't want to raise them. Some people couldn't afford it."

She sighed. "Then I won't raise them. No one will know, or care, that we charge new people more." She pointed at the almost identical bungalows across the street. "That one sold for 150K, that one for 500K. The older renters can be locked in like a fixed mortgage."

He leaned over and blew out his jack-o-lantern. "If you're in charge of it," he said. "I don't even want to review paperwork."

"You won't even know."

The next day, Meg placed a "Storage Units for Rent" sign out front. By afternoon, she had to knock off the first snow. In the bottom drawer of the file cabinet she found the contracts for the current renters—a couple sentences total, more or less a gentlemen's agreement. She went to a storage rental company and asked for their contracts and mimicked the new contracts after them. The new renters willingly paid two hundred per month.

In mid-December, they received a warning letter from the labor board. Meg showed it to her father casually on a Friday afternoon, when she usually showed him letters, bills, or emails on which she needed his advice. His brow knitted as he read. He whipped the paper to his side when he finished. "I bet Aaron contacted them after he quit," he said. "What a prick."

"What are we going to do?" She was not going to feel badly for him. He had to have known this was coming. He had to have known he couldn't *not* pay overtime forever.

"If it's Aaron he won't know whether we pay or not," he said.

"The letter says the labor board could demand our records anytime."

"They don't have time to deal with all that."

She waited for his decision, knowing he'd never allow her to make it.

"You'd think they'd go after larger companies," he continued. "Not pick on the small ones. We're just trying to keep our head above water."

Maybe, she thought, if you'd buy new equipment we'd be more productive. Yesterday the workers had waited for two hours for Enrique to fix the linker. It had broken two weeks ago, too.

"You'll see how it is when you run the business," he said. He placed the letter on her desk. "Let's pay overtime. But if anyone is getting close to forty, I'll let them out early on Friday. Can you keep track through the week?"

She said she could. She turned away, ready to finish her work and get home.

Behind her, her father paced, swearing that "the labor board has it coming," whatever that meant. She was just glad his anger wasn't directed at her.

On her way out, she heard him in the spice room on the back of the first floor. She stepped toward him to say goodbye. Through the frame of the doorway, she saw him holding a tin cup with one hand, pushing off salt with a butter knife to exact the measurement with the other. He poured the salt in the bowl, then ran a gloved finger over his father's recipe sheet that Meg had laminated. She wanted to comfort him—to say that paying a few hours of overtime wouldn't stretch them too much—but as he dipped a cup into the cinnamon jug, she turned away.

The following weekend, Meg and Caleb stayed at a cabin near Grand Lake. They traveled into the Rockies every December for a winter getaway and because Meg wanted to experience more snow than the Front Range offered in early winter. This year, she was pleased with the three feet of it. Mornings, they cross-country skied, and afternoons and evenings, they sat in front of the fire, reading or talking. One night, Caleb surprised Meg, unveiling the drawing of their future home, a nine-hundred-square-foot, three-bedroom house, with two bedrooms upstairs and one down. Meg loved the large windows, and Caleb pointed out the adjacent shop.

"Now that I'm getting paid overtime, maybe we can add an even larger window in the front room," she joked.

"You've never worked overtime."

"Maybe I'll start." She grinned and they kissed overtop of the plan.

Caleb scrunched his face. "We might have enough for a larger window somewhere. We'd have to redraw—"

She touched his hand. "It's wonderful. I love it."

She led Caleb to the couch. The fire, filled to the brim,

crackled. She said she couldn't believe she'd gotten away with reporting on her dad.

"Can you guys afford the new payments?" he asked.

"We're not supposed to give out overtime if we can help it."

"But will you get all the work done?"

"I think so." She leaned her head against his shoulder. "If I were in charge of the place, I'd set up a food truck in the parking lot. It's not that far from downtown."

"You'd sell breakfast food?"

"Bratwursts. As soon as we closed the shop for the day, I'd open the truck." The idea had come only then, as she stared into the flames, relaxed.

"It's a good idea." He leaned his head against hers. "Why do you have to wait till you're in charge?"

Why, indeed. She thought of his question the next morning as she skied one last time, while he opted to read in front of the fire. It was Monday, the men would be done cutting meat by now, and on to the grinder and sealer. She knew the routine, the scents, the gossip that relieved the monotony. She'd worked on the floor for two summers in high school. If her dad hadn't asked her to help with bookkeeping, she'd likely still be on the floor now.

She'd arrived at a clearing. Cabins and pines dotted the slope below, and at the bottom, Grand Lake stretched almost a mile in each direction. Most years, on their final day, she'd prance along the ice at the edge while Caleb nervously shook his head, but this year, she had decided to leave early, to get home before rush hour traffic.

It had all worked out for the best, she thought as she skied down. She'd always been good with figures, and as long as the office didn't get too cold, she enjoyed working there, talking to her dad or the workers only when they came up for lunch or their checks. If she started a food truck, it would need to be financially separate from the shop: she doubted her dad would be OK with such change, unless she ran it herself. She wouldn't mind cooking, but she wouldn't want to work the register. Maybe Matt could, to draw locals in. He knew so many people around town.

The Friday before Christmas, as she was compiling gift baskets for each employee as a present, Matt came up for coffee. "I'd rather have a thirty-minute lunch instead of a basket," he said.

She ignored him. She'd put off asking him to run the food truck not because she didn't trust him, but because, often, she hated him.

Matt repeated himself. She set down an orange. "And you think I can do something about it?"

"You got us overtime."

"Did I? And how many hours have you got from that?" One, she knew. He'd gotten only one hour of overtime. She turned to the name tags. "If you don't want the basket, I'll take yours."

"I didn't say that."

He set down his cup.

"Don't leave that here."

"What?"

"Your cup."

He looked around cluelessly, then grabbed it and tossed it.

Meg started affixing tags to the baskets. "Shouldn't you be working?" she asked.

"I'm taking a break that I'm legally allowed."

She shook her head.

"They're just cleaning tubs. We're almost done."

"Then feel free to take your basket and go."

"Oh yeah, I'm sure Gus would love that."

He sat at the table and stared into space. A few minutes later, the others clambered upstairs, joking and laughing, excited for a rare three-day weekend. They gathered the gift baskets, thanked her, and dispersed.

Gus didn't share their joy. As of Sunday, Christmas Eve, Meg's mother would be fifteen years dead. Every year, Meg tried to cheer him on that day with little success. Just thinking of another sad Christmas Eve with him made her tired, but she knew spending it with him was her duty, so she asked whether they should cook at her place or his.

"Mine, if you have time for it. I like the smell of ribs cooking."

She imagined a Christmas Eve in ten years, she and Caleb taking a couple kids to her dad's. The children played with new toys on the floor while Caleb small-talked with her dad and she made food. Maybe grandkids, the continuity of generations, would ease his grief? Christmas Eve would always be difficult for him, she thought, as he sat at his desk and went over invoices.

She sat at her desk and looked over the records for the storage units. Last month, she'd kept the money in the storage unit account, but this month, she'd moved the extra cash into her own account. She justified herself by labeling it her bonus for the idea to charge more. She'd save up for a food truck. July would be a good month to begin, if not this year, then the next one. She knew she should broach the idea with her dad, but she wanted to write a business plan first, to know exactly how much she'd need to borrow and how much she could contribute after she'd paid for wedding expenses. She put the storage unit folder below the others in her desk drawer.

"I'll see you tomorrow," she said, and stood. "Is two o'clock OK?"

He nodded absentmindedly.

She put her gift basket in her backpack, then left. It was generous of him to get the workers baskets, she thought. It was one of the only nice things he did.

That spring, she asked Nathan to man the food truck. She hadn't thought of him at first because he was a little older—fifty-three, according to his employee paperwork—but he'd lived in St. Anthony all his life, and because he was middle-aged, and Italian, he would draw in both communities.

She and Caleb ran into him at Ernesto's on the first day the restaurant placed tables outside. Nathan invited them over. She learned that he'd once gotten his barber's license but had never set up shop because of the costs and risk in running his own business.

Her food truck idea segued naturally from his story. As she described it, she felt Caleb smiling at her animation.

Nathan listened and shoveled spaghetti. He loved the idea, as Meg had hoped he would. He was always upbeat.

"Would you like to work there sometimes?" she asked on a whim.

He raised his eyebrows and touched his fingers to his chest.

"I imagine, at first, it would just be open for a couple hours each afternoon," she said. "Fifteen an hour OK?"

"Definitely."

Meg clapped her hands together. She instructed him not to tell her father.

In early June, she and Caleb had a small wedding ceremony and pig roasting at Caleb's parents' house. When Meg saw her dad in a suit she realized she hadn't seen him in one since her mother's funeral, a thought which saddened her. Although his movements were awkward, and his small talk less than gracious, she was grateful that he didn't raise his voice, and was happy that he enjoyed the roasting. He'd come out to the property the night before to dig the pig hole, and at the reception, as Caleb and his dad cut meat, he told her about a pig roasting he and her mom had attended before she was born.

Two weeks after the wedding, she found a used food truck on Craigslist for ten thousand dollars. When a mechanic confirmed it was in good-enough shape, Meg filled out paperwork for a loan. Once the loan was approved, and the food truck all but purchased, she finally told her father.

It was a hot Friday immediately following the Fourth of July. The men had returned from deliveries and left. Her dad was complaining about the lower number of orders that week. "As though they only get summer sales on the Fourth."

She told him that she'd buy bratwursts off him, that that would supplement the shop's income.

"You and Caleb can only eat so much," he said.

She breathed deeply. "I've been thinking of starting a food truck in the parking lot. Selling hot bratwursts. With your permission of course."

He was standing a few feet from her, hands on hips, looking at her as if he hadn't heard her.

She pulled a folder from the cabinet and handed it to him. "Here's the business plan."

He took the folder but didn't open it. "Don't you have enough work in the shop?" he asked. "I could give you more to do."

She looked into his face. Too deeply creased for a man of fifty-five. Eyes that, during a confrontation, always looked away. "I'll do more if you need me to. But this is something else. Something separate."

She caught a sadness in his glance before he avoided her gaze. He held out the folder. "Then that's your affair."

The business plan was so orderly. She'd wanted him to read it. "I'd need to use the parking lot."

"No one else is using it."

She didn't know what else to say. Her adrenaline was high; she'd expected a confrontation, or at least a discussion.

"Just let me know how many twenty-pound boxes you'll need each week," he said.

Caleb thought her dad's response was positive, but she wasn't so sure. "He doesn't seem to care either way," she said. She'd picked up a Papa Murphy's pizza on the way home, and they were standing in the kitchen, waiting for it to bake, drinking beer.

"It's better than him opposing it," Caleb said.

"Maybe." She'd expected her father to be angry but hoped for his approval. She didn't understand why he might feel hurt.

She finalized the food truck transaction that weekend. Over the next month, she was busy filing for permits, making improvements, and locking down suppliers. The money from the storage units came in handy for burnt-orange exterior touch-up paint and to order a sign. Bratwurst Heaven she called it, but had to request a redo when they sent her a sign that said "Bratwurst Haven" instead.

At the same time, the foundation was being laid on their house. She loved to come to the site in the evenings, with the bright summer light fading behind the snow-capped Rockies, and walk hand in hand with Caleb around the burgeoning structure. Unlike the food truck, she wasn't overseeing it, and didn't have to worry that something would go wrong, and if it did, whether she had the knowledge, money, or time to fix it.

She opened the food truck Labor Day weekend, hoping she might catch tourists. She and Nathan worked inside the truck on that first day, while Caleb and Pete waited for brats at the counter. An acquaintance had dropped by to take photos for the local paper. Her father, as usual on weekends, made himself scarce. She could have invited him. But he knew she was opening that day. If he wanted to drop by, he would.

"I'll take four to go," Pete said. "Buffs game today."

She hadn't considered that most people would be at home watching football. They sold only ten that Saturday but tripled their sales on Sunday. On Labor Day, Meg brought three friends and Nathan ran the stand alone. He did fine; it was basically a glorified hot dog stand, though they also sold a side of salad, chips, or fries. She wanted to eventually serve soup, but she knew that would take more prep.

The food truck's sales exceeded her expectations in September and October, but in November, when the snow arrived, people didn't want to wait outside for food. She'd expected a drop-off, but the decline was so drastic that she closed the truck on Mondays and Tuesdays and gave Nathan permission to close early whenever he deemed fit. She thought that if she got the soup underway, and maybe for winter moved the truck near the library and skating rink downtown, business would pick up, but she didn't have time to act on these ideas because she and Caleb were moving into their house.

They spent weekends in November and early December painting it. A golden living room, dark red kitchen and dining area, navy-blue bedroom. When she gave her father a tour, he said he liked the variety of colors. She asked him, while showing off the wood-burning stove, if he'd like to do Christmas Eve there this year, and he said he'd rather do it as his place. It wasn't worth arguing over, she thought. She'd offer again next year.

In early January, as a belated Christmas present to herself, she asked two contractors to give estimates on replacing the three window panes in the factory office. Her dad, who didn't know they were coming, followed them upstairs. After the second guy left, he told her that he had a friend in Edmont who replaced windows.

"I'd be happy to get an estimate from him," she said.

"I might just use him."

"If he does good work for a decent price . . ."

"We hadn't discussed that the windows need replaced."

"I order the spices without discussion."

"This is different."

It was not a routine cost; although he had to have noticed the coldness seeping in, she understood what he meant. "Yes," she said. "OK. I should have asked. Replacing them will save on the heating bill."

"I'll give Robert a call at lunch."

He then went downstairs and yelled at Honey for standing around.

His outbursts toward the workers had increased, she thought, or maybe she'd just become more sensitive. She and her dad touched base sometimes at the end of Mondays or Tuesdays, but on Wednesdays through Fridays, she came in before the other employees and finished her own work early so she could prep food in the truck. Maybe he was angry at her for not being around as much, and verbally abused the workers instead of her. She felt badly they had to take it, but didn't know what she could do.

In February, her dad coughed up phlegm for two weeks, then, one Saturday at the food truck, Nathan said he'd seen him Friday night sitting hatless on a bench on Main Street. Surprisingly to her, when she called and offered to take him to the doctor, he complied. He'd come down with pneumonia, and told Meg that until he returned to work she was in charge.

She'd just made lentil-sausage soup, one of her many soup experiments. She asked if he wanted some.

"Don't worry after me," he said.

"I have plenty."

"Why don't you drop it off after work tomorrow? Don't make an extra trip."

The next morning she told the other employees that her dad was sick and that she'd be working on the floor. She'd forgotten gloves, and after an hour, her hands were so cold that she stood aside with them tucked into the sleeves of her sweatshirt. Enrique offered her an extra pair.

After work she drove to her dad's. He was sitting in his recliner watching *Cheers*. His pale face turned toward her as she entered. "How'd it go?" he asked.

She gave him a play by play while warming soup on the stove. "I have some gloves in the garage that might fit you better than Enrique's," he said at one point. And, at another, "When Honey stands around, tell her to break down boxes or wash tubs."

He said he wasn't hungry, but when he finally ate, he ate quickly. "It's good soup. I didn't know you made soup."

"I'm trying out different types. For the food truck." As she described her plan, his eyes returned to the TV. She faded out before she shared that she wanted to snag a meeting with the guy who owned the rink.

"I'll give you a call tomorrow at the shop," he said when she paused. "Today, I'd fallen asleep."

She wouldn't discuss the truck anymore with her dad, she decided on her drive home. He didn't seem that interested in it.

On Thursday, after three days of burning her tongue on microwaved soup, she told the other employees they could have a thirty-minute break. "I must've eaten faster when I worked here in high school," she told Nathan. "I don't remember feeling so rushed."

"My doc said eating slower would help me take off weight," Nathan said, patting his stomach. "I laughed. I'm sure *he* has an hour lunch."

The following Tuesday, when she was hurrying to print out the paychecks so she could get back to the floor, Matt asked her for a ten-minute break in the morning. "We get here before six and don't have lunch till noon," he said.

"Fine, fine. Let's take one at 8:30—or whenever we finish cutting meat. But only until my dad gets back."

The rest of the week, during their ten-minute, she smoked with Carlos, Nathan, Matt, and Pete out front. They asked her how the food truck was going, and when Pete found out that she hadn't had luck in meeting with Howard Mann, the owner of the skating rink and its adjacent parking lot, he pulled out his phone. "I'll text him," he said. "He's my cousin."

Meg blinked, not believing her luck.

Almost every afternoon she took soup to her father. By the second Monday, he wasn't coughing as much and his color had returned. She was surprised he took a whole second week off, when, before his pneumonia, as far as she could remember, he'd never taken off one day. She thought he was milking the sickness, but didn't mind. He deserved time off, and they all deserved time away from him.

On Friday, she brought over the box of her mom's letters and cards. When she told him what was in it, he wouldn't look toward it. "I don't need that stuff. She's in here." He touched his forehead.

"There might be something you want to save, that you forgot about . . ."

"No." He was staring at the screen. "Feel free to take what you want and toss the rest."

While he drank Busch and chuckled at *Wings*, she went through the box. Mostly cards to her, some letters to her dad, some old school drawings. She tossed her dad's letters and the drawings but kept the cards. She liked how they were all signed *Love, Mom*.

After an hour, she rose to go.

"I'll see you in the shop on Monday then," he said.

"Yes."

"The soup helped me. Thank you."

"You're welcome. If you want more, I'll soon be selling it at the food truck."

On Monday, Meg worked hard in the office, able to tune out floor talk and her father's yelling, until the afternoon, when he stormed upstairs.

She looked up.

"You were giving them a thirty-minute lunch and a ten?" he said.

She tensed. Matt. It had to have been Matt. "Now that you're here, they can go back," she said.

"Lazy pieces of shit. Now they think I owe them."

She heard someone on the stairs. Matt stepped out. He held his bump cap and had his baseball cap pulled low. "You do owe us," he said. "One thirty-minute break and two fifteens."

"You get what I say you get."

"The labor board disagrees."

"You're the one who reported on me, aren't you?"

Meg willed Matt not to look toward her. She knew he suspected.

"Just give us a thirty-minute lunch," Matt said. "We don't need the fifteens."

"You don't need a thirty."

"I won't work for less."

"You think I need you."

"Yeah, I think you do."

Gus snorted.

Matt set down the bump cap. He looked toward Meg, as though asking her to stick up for him. She didn't look away, but didn't speak. He pulled off his apron and dropped it on the floor. "I quit." He turned and headed downstairs. Seconds later, he opened and closed the large front door.

"Jesus," Gus said. "What an idiot." He was almost growling. He turned to Meg. "I'll need to help downstairs. We'll talk later."

She tried to get back to the paperwork but couldn't focus. She unloaded a delivery of spices and took them to the spice room. Enrique was there, measuring. She set the packages under the counter. "Ira tomar algo con nosotros hoy?" he asked.

"Maybe," she said. They'd never invited her to get a drink.

"Eres una buena jefa," he said.

She nodded a thanks at his praise.

At the end of the day, as her father approached, she was sitting at her desk, looking down, shaking. "I told you they could go back to a twenty," she said.

"You think I don't know how to run a business," he said.

She folded her fingers together and looked at them. "You left me in charge."

"I wanted you to run the place as I've been running it."

"They get tired."

He smirked. "Oh I'm sure, for you, they pretended to be tired."

She stood up and loaded her backpack. "I also got tired. And I wanted a longer lunch too."

"You don't know how to run a business after six months."

She clenched her jaw.

"Eleven years, and I haven't gone bankrupt."

She zipped the bag and slid on the straps. "Is that the goal, to not go bankrupt?"

"What other goal is there?"

She looked at him. "To run a good business, to do well."

"That ship's sailed."

"Why? Didn't grandpa do better?"

"A different era."

"Eleven years ago was a different era?"

"He died right as the recession began. We lost lots of clients. They didn't want to pay more for small and local."

She bet they didn't want to deal with her father's belligerence. She folded her arms.

"How's your business doing?" he asked.

She raised her chin. Thanks to Pete, she was meeting with Howard Mann on Wednesday. But she wasn't going to share that.

"Not well?" he said.

She tightened the straps on her pack. "It's fine. And it'll do better when summer comes around."

"If you need help, just ask."

She squinted at him. She had no idea he was willing to help.

"I can show you how to skirt the law," he said. "Sometimes, to get by, you need to break rules."

She thought of the money from the storage units. Her dad was the law she was skirting. She had no problem with business rules. "I won't do anything to hurt my employees."

"There are other, legal loopholes, too."

Suddenly, she was tired and angry. "If you treated them better, you wouldn't have as high turnover."

"If you aren't strict they won't give you respect."

"You don't have to yell."

"If you think you can tell me how to run this place, you better be looking for another job."

"Are you threatening to fire me?"

"I'm warning you."

"You're gonna fire me for saying people shouldn't be yelled at?"

"I'm not firing you."

She walked far to the side of him and padded down the stairs. Outside, she texted Caleb that she was going for a drink. She left her pickup in front of the shop because she felt like walking through snow. Flakes whipped around her. She saw her breath. She passed houses that smelled like fire, and, looking up, saw chimneys breathing smoke.

Inside Fred's was very quiet. She sat at the counter. She recognized the bartender, Cynthia. They'd played soccer together in high school.

Meg ordered a toddy. She looked toward the dartboards to make sure none of the workers were there.

Cynthia set the drink across the counter. "Sometimes they go to another bar first."

Meg wrapped her cold hands around the hot glass. She wanted to cry. She wanted to quit. She wanted to go back to the shop and yell at her dad. She'd tell him how easily she'd taken the storage unit money. She'd tell him she was sick of being his work horse and mother.

"How's Caleb these days?" Cynthia asked.

"He's good."

"Always was a sweetheart. Not surprised you guys got together."

Meg stirred the toddy. Steam caressed her face. She thought of that fall, when she'd suggested to Caleb that they skip their Grand Lake trip because of work, and he'd convinced her to go, saying that they hadn't had enough time together since she'd started the food truck. It was amazing how well they talked through things, that she had confidence he listened to her.

"And how's that food truck? Matt was telling me about it. Bratwurst Heaven, right?"

Meg nodded.

"Matt's a handful, right?"

"Yeah. The truck's doing OK. I think it'll do better in the summer. Got some regulars."

Cynthia swung over to chat with a guy down the counter. By the time she returned, only a dollop of honey remained in Meg's glass. Cynthia set dishes in the sink, plugged it, and turned on the hot water.

The pressure in Meg's head had become an ache in her chest.

Cynthia turned. "You have a sign for your food truck?"

Meg nodded.

"Is the exterior painted? I've painted murals in Boulder. I could paint it."

Meg tried to think of a fitting design. Steam rose from the sink.

"It's fine if you're done with it," Cynthia said.

Why not let her take a look? She might have some good ideas. Meg felt hopeful for the first time that day. "It can always be improved," she said.

The crew started filing in. First Pete, then Carlos, then Enrique, then Nathan. There were seven or eight in all. Nathan spotted Meg, came over, and offered to buy her a drink. "What a day," he said.

Meg agreed, thanked him, and ordered another toddy. She chatted with him about the food truck while Cynthia made Meg's drink, then filled two pitchers of Coors Light for Nathan. He headed with the beer toward the guys and dart boards.

Above the bar, the news was on. "That virus thing again," Cynthia said. "Hope it's not a big deal." She switched the channel to a Nuggets game.

Meg asked whether she was serious about painting the truck.

"For sure. You have any ideas? I could paint a scene, like with people or a landscape, or just make it colorful."

Bratwurst Heaven, Meg thought. So maybe a portrait of angels making brats? She almost smiled. One of these days, not so long from now, earlier than she thought this morning, she'd leave the factory, and her father would run it into the ground. He'd sell off the acre to pay debts, to fund retirement—he was lucky the land sat in a gentrifying area, not some small, stagnant, or declining, formerly industrial Midwestern town. A company would build condos, she imagined, after leveling the factory building.

"Have you ever been in the factory?" Meg asked. "Or just looked inside?"

"Didn't want to, with that scent coming off them."

Now Meg really smiled. "Maybe I can take you in there," she said. "Sometime my dad isn't around. And you could see what it looks like, with people working in it, and paint a scene of that on the truck."

"A slice of heaven?"

"Maybe I mean it ironically."

"Yeah," Cynthia said, "I could do that."

"How much do you charge?"

Cynthia waved a hand. "Let's talk about that after the tour, after I see the food truck."

They exchanged numbers.

A couple ordered a pitcher of Coors Light, but the keg kicked as Cynthia filled it, so she offered it to Meg.

"I'll take it to the guys," Meg said.

At the round table, Enrique was talking about his Denver delivery route in Spanish, while Pete listened and Carlos interjected. Meg topped off all three of their glasses, then sat down. If she concentrated, she could understand what Enrique said. There was this new manager at one of the chains who didn't want to pay in cash, and Enrique told him to take it up with Gus, but the manager wouldn't let up on Enrique. "I'll go there with you next time," Carlos said in English. "Then we'll see what he says."

It was always the same bullshit, Meg thought, and drank the rest of the beer straight out of the pitcher. When she lowered it and saw the guys looking over at her in surprise, she started laughing. She didn't know why. Then all four of them were laughing at her and at themselves and at the factory, and it felt good to be there laughing at something, together, even briefly, while the world continued to do whatever it would do, outside.